PRAISE FOR DEBRA PARMLEY

"Parmley's book, the 17th in the 50-book American Mail Order Brides series, is a creditable edition to the series and is sure to keep fans engaged....Parmley does a good job crafting characters whom readers will be eager to see succeed, and she keeps the plot moving with some unexpected twists and a good helping of suspense."

- Bridget Keown - RT Book Reviews

"It's been quite a while since this reviewer had to re-read a book because she was so involved with the story that she forgot to take notes! Isabella takes you on a wonderful, exciting ride full of intrigue, adventure, and ending with an HEA."

- Kitty Lane - Affaire deCoeur magazine

ISABELLA BRIDE OF OHIO

AMERICAN MAIL ORDER BRIDES

DEBRA PARMLEY

Copyright © 2015 by Debra Parmley and Robert Arrow

Cover Art Copyright by Belo Dia Publishing Inc. © 2021

Published in the United States of America

Fourth Edition Large Print Publish Date: February 2022

This fourth edition is a sweeter version of the story for large print.

Editor: Tamara Hoffa

Cover Artist: Sheri McGathy

All rights reserved. No portion of this book may be reproduced or transmitted in any form or by any electronic or mechanical means, including photocopying, recording or by any information retrieval and storage system without permission of the publisher. E-books are not transferrable, either in whole or in part. As the purchaser or otherwise lawful recipient of an e-book, you have the right to enjoy the novel on your own computer or other device. Further distribution, copying, sharing, gifting or uploading is illegal and violates United States Copyright laws. Pirating of eBooks is illegal. Criminal Copyright Infringement, including infringement without monetary gain, may be investigated by the Federal Bureau of Investigation and is punishable by up to five years in federal prison and a fine of up to $250,000.

Names, characters and incidents depicted in this book are products of the author's imaginations, or are used in a fictitious situation. Any resemblances to actual events, locations, organizations, incidents or persons – living or dead – are coincidental and beyond the intent of the authors.

Belo Dia Publishing Inc.

2966 Elmore Park Rd. #341125

Memphis, TN 38134

TABLE OF CONTENTS

DEDICATION FROM DEBRA:

This book is dedicated to my paternal grandmother, Isabella Ragnhild Milner, whose parents were from Sweden.

I was excited to receive the invitation to write in the American Mail Order Bride series. It's been an honor and a blessing to be able to pay homage to my home state of Ohio and Yellow Springs, the old stomping grounds near my home town, as well as to be able to bring a bit of my grandmother and her Swedish background to life within these pages.

FROM ROBERT:

Everything Debra said. I also want to thank God and her for this amazing opportunity and my family and friends for their unending love and encouragement. Finally, thanks, Becky for those last minute thoughts. ;)

ISABELLA BRIDE OF OHIO, AMERICAN MAIL ORDER BRIDE

By
Debra Parmley and Robert Arrow

CHAPTER ONE

SEPTEMBER 1890, LAWRENCE, MASSACHUSETTS

Here in America nothing lasts.

Isabella Britta Stolt stood with her four friends Lilly, Tabitha, Hope and Trinity as she glanced around at the other women gathered in the small park on the banks of the Merrimack River.

The women had gathered to hear what Roberta McDaniel, their former mill manager had to say. The Brown Textile Mill on Canal Street had employed every one of them, like her, until the fire a week ago, which had changed everything when the building burned down to the ground.

Nothing lasts.

Isabella had lost both her parents right before moving to Lawrence, Massachusetts two months before. Right after arriving at Ellis Island on the boat from Sweden which brought them to America along with the illness that had taken her parents lives.

Nothing lasts. Grandmother always said trouble comes in threes. Every time someone Grandmother knew went to heaven, she would start counting.

But Isabella had no family left to lose.

The fire would be three.

She could only pray that it was the last of her troubles.

Isabella had dreamed a repeat of the fire last night, after knocking over a candle in the kitchen, which had caught a towel on fire. Such a small fire compared to the events of that night, but it had been enough to bring on the dream. She needed comfort today.

She'd dreamed she was back working in the factory, on the fifth floor.

The clanging and the banging of equipment, which rang throughout the enormous room twenty four hours a day drowned out any sounds coming from outside the factory. Keeping her head down as usual, concentrating on her sewing and hoping Mr. Brown would not stand near her again, leering and trying to touch her, Isabella brushed back a lock of hair that had fallen down from her Swedish braids and sewed the next seam.

Her father's Bible lay on her lap and she'd placed her left hand upon it when she felt Mr. Brown cast his gaze over to her.

Her hand pressed against the worn leather as his gaze pressed down upon her, making her feel squeamish. She peered at him beneath lowered lids, not wanting to fully look at the man who appeared to her as if he could be the devil himself with his slicked back hair as black as coal and his pointed Van Dyke beard.

Though he wore a suit, and as the owner of the factory was respected in this town, she disliked and distrusted him.

His gaze lingered and then shifted as Roberta McDaniel walked up to him. He turned his attention to her and away from Isabella, who was forgotten for now.

She returned her attention to her sewing and away from the potbellied man in the fancy suit, hoping this was the end of his attention today.

With so many women in the factory, why does he keep singling me out? There are nearly six hundred people who work here, most of them women. Yet his gaze always finds me.

She watched as Roberta climbed the steps up to the upper room, where the manager's office was.

Mr. Brown made his way over to Isabella and her hand found the Bible again.

What does he want?

It looks as if he has something to say to me. Please God make him go away and leave me alone.

This time her prayer was answered, and soon he mounted the stairs, and headed to the manager's office to meet with Roberta.

It wasn't long after Mr. Brown and Roberta McDaniel met in the office that Mr. Brown left the building.

He'd paused once more, looking at her with the strangest expression before he'd turned suddenly and left.

Isabella breathed a sigh of relief and pushed her hair back out of her face again.

Today the heat in the building was worse than usual, strange for September. The air was stifling, and the noise unrelenting.

Isabella wished her shift would end soon, a wish, which would be granted with the setting of the sun just now past the many windows, which lined the factory walls.

She worked from just before the sun came up until just after it went down. The only time she saw the sun was through the factory windows, unless it was her day off.

The fire had come so suddenly, the heat in the building rising. There had been a crash as windows were broken. Flames spread, licking up the walls like giant tongues of fire as thick smoke rolled across the factory floor.

Women started to scream and rose from their sewing machines en masse to turn and run, trying to find their way out. Isabella grabbed her Bible and ran with them.

The first door closest to them, which she and several other women raced toward was locked tight.

Did he mean to lock us in?

"Gud nej," God, no, she screamed. *How will we get out*?

Lilly heard Isabella and hurried to her side. "Come," she said. "This way."

She ran with Lilly to another door, at the opposite end of the cavernous room, which wasn't locked, and they raced down the stairs among the other women who rushed down the stairs and out of the building into the fresh air.

Thick smoke was now pouring out of the windows and machinery crashed through the floors as the flames devoured the wooden planks. The sight of the huge factory filled with flames blazed into Isabella's sight as one she would never forget.

"What a horrible accident," a woman cried. "I hope everyone gets out."

"Jag tror inte det," Isabella said.

Lilly turned to look at her sharply, "You don't believe it was an accident?"

"No, I do not."

"Why do you say that?"

"Because I saw Mr. Brown leave early and he gave me the strangest look before he went out that door which was locked. I think he didn't want anyone following him. Not long afterward the fire began."

Lilly raised surprised brows. "You think he started it?"

"Yes. I do." Isabella nodded.

"He is a horrible man. I'm glad you won't have to fend off any more of his advances. But it's best you don't say any more about Mr. Brown. You don't want to draw his attention."

They stood with the other women watching the factory that was their livelihood burn down.

Fire engines hurried to put the flames out, but the flames were too large and the factory was too far-gone to save it.

~

Now Isabella stood at the park near the riverbank, remembering the fire and wondering why Roberta McDaniel had called them here today.

Roberta was speaking to the ladies about a mail order bride matchmaker.

Isabella turned her attention fully to Roberta.

"My sister recently went to Kansas as a mail order bride, and she's written to me how happy she is with her groom. A matchmaker in Beckman found her future husband for her.

I went to see this matchmaker yesterday to find out if she had any other prospective grooms and she gave me the newest edition of the Grooms' Gazette, listing men from all over the United States who are looking for brides. She gave me fifty copies, so if you're interested in being a mail order bride, please come forward."

Yes, I can do this and when I marry, I will wear Mother's wedding dress.

Isabella pictured the beautiful dress packed in her steamer trunk.

The ladies began murmuring among themselves.

Roberta was passing out copies of a newspaper

called the Grooms' Gazette—where men from all over the country advertised for wives.

"I'll get copies for us," Hope said as she turned to walk toward Roberta.

Hope moved to the front of the crowd, took a few copies of the paper from Roberta, and moved back to the small huddle of friends. "Here's one for each of us," Hope said as she handed a newspaper to each of them.

But Tabitha wouldn't take the paper when Hope held it out to her.

"I don't know if I could do this. I'd be scared to death I'd end up with a mean man." Tabitha shook her head again to Hope's offer. "I have enough savings to get me to my cousin's home in Missouri."

Isabella noticed Hope biting her lip as if holding back what she wanted to say about Tabitha's relation.

Lilly opened the newspaper and began reading. Lilly, like Isabella, had come from Sweden. She had been in America for two years and when Isabella arrived to take the factory job, Lilly had taken her under her wing and become her roommate and confidant.

Often Isabella had watched Lilly to see what to do next at the factory in the two weeks since she had taken the job and now she fell into that pattern again, as if she were following an older sister's lead.

Lilly was outgoing and outspoken where Isabella was quiet and shy, still working on confidence in her English speaking ability.

Now she cleared her throat and spoke up. "Father tried to arrange a marriage for me before he decided to bring us to America," Isabella said, "but the boy had another girl in mind. Without father . . ."

Her words and gaze drifted off as if thinking of him. Then she spoke again, more decisive now. "Father would have had any suitor investigated." She reached for the paper and nodded. "That is what I will do. I will make sure he is a good man before I marry him."

"Sign up to be someone's wife, not knowing who this person is? I don't know what to think of the idea." Lilly frowned.

"What will you all do in the meantime while we wait to hear from these men?" Hope asked.

"I should be able to leave right away," Tabitha said. "I'm already packed, and all that remains is to buy my ticket."

"There's a family in town that is in need of a house-maid," Isabella said. "But only for one month. Their maid just had a baby and she will return. The baker's wife helped me get the job. I'm to start tomorrow."

"I've always talked my way into finding odds and ends jobs, be it cleaning fish or scrubbing laundry, so I know I can continue to scrape by . . . until I find me a groom to pay my way out of this city," Lilly said with a sly smile, looking around at her circle of friends.

Hope nodded.

"Hope, you haven't told us what you're going to do while you wait to hear back," Tabitha said.

"That's because I don't know," Hope replied with a forced joviality. "I'm about to have a great adventure, I suppose."

"Nothing lasts here in America," Isabella said. "I haven't even been here a year and now I must move again, a third time. I don't know what the future holds or what is best, but I pray it will be good and that it will last. Adventures can be full of danger, Hope. I will pray for all of us to be safe and healthy."

"I'll figure it out," Hope said, waving off their concern. "I appreciate it, I really do, but I'll be all right."

"So how does this work? Do we write to each person?" Lilly asked.

"I think you'd pick a few who might interest

you, and start with them. Where would you want to live? Is there a man's profession you'd feel comfortable with?"

"I'd like to go somewhere there are more Swedes than here in Massachusetts. And more open country rather than the stifling smell of this factory town," Isabella said in Swedish to Lilly.

Isabella had only been in America for three months, arriving in New York then traveling to the Boston area to find work. Her time living alone in New York City, waiting on her parents to recover and be released from quarantine and after they passed had been overwhelming.

Now she longed for the fresh country air and the quieter feeling of safety in a smaller town.

Although Isabella worked diligently to learn English, she lapsed back to her native tongue when stressed.

"I've heard there are more Swedish settlements in Minnesota, Illinois or Kansas than here in the Northeast. I wonder what the weather is out West?" Lilly said in English so the others could understand.

Isabella blushed realizing she'd lapsed once again into speaking only Swedish which was so easy with Lilly.

"Surely it's not any worse than the northeasters

we've experienced last winter. I think I'd prefer to go south if I had a choice," Trinity said.

"Okay, let's go back to our apartment and pick out who we want to write to. We'll never get husbands standing around here feeling sorry for ourselves," Hope said as she picked up her skirt and started walking across the grassy park.

Lilly looked around at the women leaving the park or still talking in groups.

Isabella, noting this, glanced around and wondered how many of these women Lilly would miss. Though Isabella was too new to the factory to have grown close to any but her roommate and their three friends, Lilly had been there much longer.

"It is like a painting, such moments," Isabella said. "Never to come again."

These were all good women. Though Isabella didn't know them well, having only worked at the factory for two weeks, she knew that much. They were good women who worked hard and only wanted to improve their lives.

That feeling came over her again, the nostalgic feeling of loss and impermanence.

Here in America nothing lasts. Moments were to be savored and treasured, for they would not come again.

Lilly, never one to encourage Isabella's lapses into melancholy brought on by missing her parents, linked her arm into Isabella's as they walked out of the park. "Come on, Isabella, it's time us Swedish girls find two rich American husbands."

Isabella smiled and said, "Yes, I am ready."

~

"I BELIEVE I have found one gentleman to write to. Here is the advertisement he placed," Isabella read from the paper.

She'd read the advertisements for mail order brides through three times, thinking over what the men had written.

"To the dear ladies looking to find a husband;

I am a thirty-seven year old man of not inconsiderable means looking to find a wife for whom to provide a decent, honest living.

I am six foot, two inches tall and not terribly thin, but certainly not running to fat. The black in my hair has not yet begun to gray, and my brown eyes are still sharp. I am an accountant by trade, with a small home out in the country near Yellow Springs, Ohio. Any interested lady may apply."

She glanced up from her paper over to Lilly. "A small home out in the country is just the kind of home I wish to live in. Mr. Donald Jenks is much older than I, but he sounds established and solid. I don't want to have to move again should something happen."

"He sounds like a good choice." Lilly nodded.

"I will write to him then. Help me?" Without realizing it, she had lapsed into Swedish again.

Lilly put her hand over Isabella's and answered her in English. "Yes, I will help you."

"Thank you. I do not want to sound too much like a new immigrant. He might prefer a woman who is better at English."

"Isabella, your English is fine and it is getting better every day. You just have not had as much practice as some. He may find you enchanting, with your soft Swedish voice. I know listening to you sing makes me smile," Lilly said.

"Yes, but you understand me in Swedish and in English," Isabella said.

"He will learn to understand you too," Lilly said. "Come I will help you write the letter."

STANDING IN CHURCH, singing the hymns was a comfort to Isabella. The familiarity of the hymns' tunes took Isabella back to their old church in Orby, Alvsborg Sweden; to remembering father's booming voice as he sang beside her and mother's silent lip singing of the words, for mother could not hold a tune.

Isabella's voice was neither booming like her father's nor tuneless like her mother's. Soft and sweet, Isabella's was the perfect voice to sing children to sleep.

Though she'd taken the job with the Petersons as a housemaid, having heard her sing, she was now also the one to lull their three children to sleep at night.

There, in the nursery, she would sing softly, watching as the children's eyes drifted closed. She would dream of having her own children to sing to.

Today she sang out in church, remembering her father and feeling as if he were right beside her, offering that booming voice and the strength of his support.

Hoping she was doing the right thing, she had sent out the letter to Mr. Donald Jenks.

Good luck and God willing, she would soon be on her way to a little country house in Yellow Springs, Ohio.

It was time to sing a little louder and be brave.

CHAPTER 2

Sitting back down after singing the last hymn, Isabella thought about the letter she had sent.

She wondered how Mr. Donald Jenks would respond.

It had taken her several tries to compose it, having crumpled up three of them and it wasn't until Lilly had announced the last one perfect that Isabella had felt confident enough to send it to him.

Her thoughts now returned to the letter.

Dear Mr. Donald Jenks,

I am answering your advertisement in the Grooms' Gazette for a mail order bride.

My name is Isabella Britta Stolt. I am seventeen years old, soon to be eighteen, and I am from Sweden.

I am one hundred sixty centimeters tall with blonde hair and blue eyes, and am a small boned woman, neither too thin, nor overly round.

Currently I am living in Lawrence, Massachusetts and was working at the Brown Textile Mill until a week ago when a fire destroyed the building.

My parents are deceased and as I have no other living relatives, I have no wish to return to Sweden.

I have some modest funds remaining and a temporary job for the next month. Then I must decide what to do next. I have not been in America long, but I am practicing my English every day. Father was an engineer and I grew up surrounded by books, which gave me a love of reading.

The city life is not for me. I wish to live in a small home out in the country such as you have described. To be where there are trees, flowers and birds singing sweetly and to be able to watch the stars at night.

I wish to live in a good place to raise children. I would like to learn more about your country home. Do you hope to have children?

What more do you look for in a wife? I am an excellent hand at sewing and love to embroider. I am a good cook.

Please tell me more about yourself. I look forward

to getting to know you and I look forward to your reply.

Sincerely, Isabella Britta Stolt

Now that she'd sent the letter, there was nothing to do but to wait and pray. She turned her attention back to the service to listen to the sermon after sending up one small prayer.

Please God, let my husband be a good man.

Roberta McDaniel had said it could take a month before Isabella would know whether she and Mr. Donald Jenks suited each other.

The best thing to do was to stay busy, and thankfully, this was not difficult, for her work at the Petersons as a house-maid, which now also included tucking the children in at night, sped her days right along.

Then one day, a letter from Mr. Donald Jenks arrived.

Isabella could hardly wait to open it. She tore it open quickly, unfolding the letter and reading as fast as her eyes could race across the page.

My dear Isabella,

May I just begin by saying how delighted I am to receive your letter.

I was beginning to think no one wanted anything to do with a crusty, old accountant!

From your description of yourself, you sound absolutely lovely.

I must admit, however, to having done a bit of research on conversion tables, as I had no idea how tall one hundred sixty centimeters is! After asking around a bit, though, I believe I have worked out your height to be about five foot, three inches.

To answer your next question, I believe mine is close to one hundred eighty-eight centimeters.

What a pair we shall make when people see us!

I do offer my condolences, both for your parents and the unfortunate happenings of your old job.

On the other hand, I am very glad that you are not without some means of living for a while.

Hopefully, I will be able to aid in such endeavors.

Your words of living in the country warm my heart. I too have a passion in the soothing power of country life.

I cannot but help imagine raising children someday, with the same wide-eyed delight in the out-of-doors that you and I seem to share.

As far as what I look for in a good wife, I believe you have hit the proverbial nail on the head, my sweet. I would like for her to be able to sew and cook, as you do.

Of course she must have a good nature about her

and an amiable personality that gets along well with others.

As for myself, I am afraid you are corresponding with a simple man. I enjoy the outdoors, as I stated earlier, but I can also be found with my nose in a ledger, working late into the evening.

The only vices I allow myself are the occasional cigar and snifter of brandy.

I am not a card-player, nor do I encourage the uncertainty of gambling and chance.

People have told me before that I am a good violinist, though to my own ears, I am frightfully inexperienced.

I hope this goes some way towards satisfying your request for learning about me.

Perhaps we can exchange more information in our next letters. Wouldn't want to give away too much too soon, now, would we?

Like you, I look forward to your reply.

Again, thank you, Donald Jenks

She finished reading the letter and clasped it to her breast as happy tears formed in her eyes.

Oh it is all so wonderful. He is wonderful. I must write to him straight away.

She reached for a sheet of paper and began,

Dear Mr. Donald Jenks,

I am so happy to receive your wonderful letter. I do

not think you are so old! On my father's side of the family the men lived well into their eighties, except for my father. I still miss him.

Thank you for sending your condolences on the loss of both of my parents and my job.

Everything has been so incredibly difficult since setting foot in America.

Oh, how I long for a peaceful, happy and stable home life. One where I am safe, cared for and happy.

It is kind of you to offer to help me with a means of living. I confess I do not have the funds to travel to you. It could take quite some time to save enough to travel that far. I have nothing by way of dowry beyond the items in my steamer trunk. I would be coming to you with only two trunks, which contain all I own in the world and myself.

My temporary job as a housemaid with the Peterson family has brought me joy, which has been a balm to my soul, as I also sing to the children at night before they go to sleep. They are such sweet, dear children. Full of such joy and love. I love singing to them.

I hope God will bless us with our own when the time is right. With your violin playing and my singing I believe our children could be delightfully musical! I would love to hear you play.

American measurements are so different than I am used to and one of the things I must adapt to for your country to become my own. I am slow, but once I figure the conversions all is well. Sometimes people misunderstand my slowness to mean I am not good at mathematics. They don't realize I am converting, doing the mathematical problems they would also be doing in my country. With your accounting work you will likely be much faster at mathematics than I, but I will catch up if you are patient with me. Oh, I am so happy you took the time to do the conversions so that we might understand each other better.

I do hope we will grow to understand each other well.

My goodness, but you are tall! We shall, as you said, make such a pair!

You have expressed your wish that your wife be of good nature and able to get along well with others. I get along well with others, though I am usually the quiet one. In fact I can be quite shy. Never prone to arguing, and I avoid gossip.

I am glad you are a simple man who enjoys the outdoors and a gentleman not overly given to vices.

If you smoke or enjoy a brandy to relax at the end of a long day, such things are common among the gentlemen of Europe. Perhaps you will find my company relaxing as well. Often in the evenings I read poetry or one of the classics and I also study my Bible. I can see us enjoying a quiet evening at home with a fire crackling in the fireplace.

There are many questions I would ask but as this letter is already quite long and I must finish it before I go to work, I will limit myself to three questions.

Do you have family living nearby? Or are you like me, without living relatives?

What church do you belong to? I was raised Lutheran and have hope of being married in the Lutheran church, wearing my mother's wedding dress.

Can you describe your home? What type of house do you have? I do hope there is a garden or that you will allow me to plant one if there is not. Planting and tending to flowers is something I enjoy and have missed since leaving Sweden.

Thank you again for your wonderful letter. I hope to hear from you soon.

Looking forward to your reply, Isabella

Closing the letter, she didn't wait for Lilly to read her reply this time. The words had flown from her heart to the page in her joy and her feelings of inadequacy had fled.

Hurrying on to the Petersons, she could not contain her happiness and fairly skipped along as thoughts of how wonderful life with Mr. Donald Jenks could be. The day sped by and soon she was tucking the children in and singing to them again.

~

Had the days flown so fast? Already there was a reply from Mr. Donald Jenks!

Isabella ripped open the thick package. “Mr. Donald Jenks has sent money.” She glanced over at Lilly. “A large sum of money.”

The largest sum of money Isabella had ever seen. She stood looking down at her hand, which held the envelope and contents. She fanned the money out without counting it and Lilly’s eyes widened.

“He is a generous man,” Lilly said. “You are fortunate.”

“Yes, he is,” Isabella said. “I had no idea.” Dazed by his generosity she shook her head.

“What does the letter say?” Lilly leaned forward as if to peer at it for herself.

Isabella pulled the letter closer to herself and angled away. “I will tell you after I have read it.”

“Well hurry then!”

Isabella unfolded the letter. “I am. Hush now while I read.”

Turning the lamp on the table up, she sat and, grinning, read his words as quickly as she could, barely slowing down to comprehend them.

Dear Isabella,

There's no need to be so formal! I do hope you look forward to meeting me as much as I do to meeting you. Already, I feel like old friends, getting to know so much about one another so fast.

To answer your questions in order: Regrettably, I have no living family remaining and, as the son of two single children, am the last of my line. Since you bring up the thought of children, I hope you won't mind me beseeching Heaven with entreaties for sons to carry on the old family name. I believe this brings me very neatly to the next point: that of church.

Unfortunately, I must disappoint you on several counts, my dear. First, I have not found so much as a single Lutheran church anywhere close to my home. Second, My parents were semi-devout Catholics who, I'm afraid, did not instill a very church-going spirit in their son.

Certainly, I have no objection if you would like to regularly attend services wherever you like. Perhaps you may even prove a good influence on this old heathen and get me back into the pew, so to speak.

My home is one of the brightest parts of my life that I think will attract you. It is a white two-story affair with a porch in front and a garden out back. As I stated in the advertisement, it is out in the country, yet is not too far to preclude a short commute as a normal workday routine. The bedrooms are both upstairs.

Downstairs there is, of course, the kitchen, a dining room, my personal study, and a parlor with a lovely fireplace for receiving visitors or relaxing at day's end.

Your vision of us spending quiet evenings together may be more prophetic than you think.

My dear, I do hope I'm not being too forward, but I must confess that I have become seized with an overwhelming desire to meet you. I simply must know if you are as wonderful as it seems, and if we can be together as I imagine we can.

I entreat, nay, beg you, to do me this one favor, though we have known of each other only a little while. Please accept this humble offering as a gift so that it may pay your way to come and be with me here, if only for a little while. You have my word of honor that should we find ourselves different beyond reconciliation, I shall finance your journey back home, or wherever you would like in the world, be it even all the way back to your childhood home in Sweden.

If I have offended, or indeed been too forward, as I fear, I offer my sincere and heartfelt apologies. Please understand, I cast no judgment upon you or any of your circumstances, but simply wish to extend a helpful hand.

As always, I eagerly await your beloved reply.

Sincerely, Donald

So hurriedly had she read his letter that his

words had barely sunk in, but caught up in the overall response of Mr. Donald Jenks she could only look over at Lilly and say, “Oh Lilly!”

“What is it dear?” Lilly reached out her hand and touched Isabella’s arm. “Tell me.”

Isabella looked at Lilly, her eyes wide with excitement. “Lilly he wants to meet me! He has sent the funds for me to go and meet him and he has even said if we did not suit each other he would pay my way back home to Sweden!”

Lilly, surprised by this news, was momentarily speechless.

The moment however did not last long and she was her bubbly self again. “Are you going to meet him?”

“Yes,” Isabella’s normally quiet voice rose with excitement. “I am. Oh Lilly, this is what I have dreamed of! Of course I am!”

She was up now, unable to sit a moment longer for her excitement and moving about the room as she spoke faster, not waiting for a response from Lilly, who seemed dumbfounded by this sudden animation from her friend.

“Oh, there is so much to do! I must buy a ticket, and tell the Petersons goodbye, and pack, and-oh,” she looked at Lilly from where she’d stopped in the middle of the room. "Why, I must write him back. Tonight!"

"I am so happy for you, dear! We must celebrate." Lilly stood and giving Isabella a hug, said, "I will get out the box of Swedish cookies I have been saving for a special occasion."

Isabella clasped her hands together and said, "That would be lovely."

Lilly gathered the cookies and two plates and placed them on the table.

They each took a cookie.

"How soon will you go?" Lilly asked before taking a bite.

"Why, just as soon as I can, of course." Isabella took one nibble of her cookie and then placed it on her plate. "I must write to him straight away."

"Well go on then, dear, go on."

"Yes." Isabella pulled out a sheet of paper and laid Mr. Donald Jenks' letter beside it.

Re-reading the letter, she paused.

Oh. There would be no Lutheran church to be married in.

Well, it is not as I had dreamed, but as long as a suitable church could be found, and a minister to perform the ceremony, I will be content with that. And if he is no longer attending a church, then he might be more amenable to attending one of my liking.

She frowned slightly.

The question of religion would have been one of the first questions father would have asked and the question would have been settled early on before his approval was given.

She pushed that thought aside.

Mr. Donald Jenks seems amenable to the idea of attending church. Otherwise, well, I would not be able to marry him.

The two former Catholics she knew seemed to have settled into Lutheranism and fit in quite well. They even said how much more relaxed the Lutheran church was.

Why, Mr. Donald Jenks might even find he enjoyed the Lutheran church.

She glanced down at his letter again.

I had hoped he might have some family living, as I have none of my own, but as long as we are happy together, that is what matters most. And he wanted children! Dear, sweet children. If he wants sons to carry on his family name, I shall do my very best and, God willing, we might fill our house with happy children.

And what a house. Why, I can close my eyes and see it now. And it has a garden!

"Well?" Lilly's voice interrupted Isabella's reveries. "If you don't write to him, I shall!"

"Oh." Startled from her runaway thoughts, her

eyes flew open and she held up her hand to her friend as if to hold her off from beginning a letter of her own. "I'm writing! I'm writing!"

Oh, I must not delay any longer with all these thoughts running through my head.

Smiling, she took another sip of sherry, took a deep breath, and began to write.

My Dear Mr. Jenks,

Far from offending or being too forward, your letter has filled me with delight and surprise such as I can hardly contain it to write this letter.

I am sure you are anticipating my response, so I must answer you straight away and not keep you waiting a moment more.

Yes, I am so looking forward to meeting you. Nothing could make me happier than I am this night with your letter and invitation. You are a most kind and generous man to offer to pay my passage back to my homeland. Far beyond what I would have ever dreamed.

Your home I believe, I have dreamed of. If it is anything like what I have pictured, then our meeting is meant to be.

If there is no Lutheran church in your hometown, it would not be possible to marry in the Lutheran church. We must then find an acceptable alternative, for we must be married in a church before God.

I do not understand these marriages, which are entered into without God's blessings upon them.

The thought of raising children, sons to carry on your family name, fills me with delight.

I wish to learn more of your family and its origins and for you to learn of mine.

Family traditions have always been important to me and I would be proud to carry yours forward.

I shall post this letter tomorrow morning and give notice to my employers, then I shall know which date I may travel to meet you.

My dearest wish is that our meeting be all that we both have dreamed and that it will happen soon.

Isabella

THE DAY HAD COME at last and Isabella's train was at the station. Her trunks had been loaded and soon it would be time for her to board. Lilly had come to see her off at the station.

"Just think. In a few weeks you will be Mrs. Hardesty and you will be singing up in Chicago and I will be Mrs. Jenks down in Yellow Springs tending my garden." Isabella smiled and dreaminess came over her as she thought of the garden. "I can hardly believe it."

"It is exciting isn't it?" Lilly tipped her head and looked at Isabella. "Are you nervous?"

"Very. It is not easy, this going off to marry a man I have never met." She wrung her gloved hands.

"No, it is not," Lilly agreed. "Isabella, I want you to promise you will come to my home if you find yourself in a bad situation; if something goes wrong with your intended."

"Yes, Lilly, I will." Isabella nodded. "I am sure everything will be fine, but I promise. Oh Lilly, you must promise me too. Things can happen so fast to change our lives forever. But our friendship will hold fast and will not change. You are like a sister to me and dear to my heart."

"Yes, I promise too. We heart sisters must stick together." Lilly eyed the waiting train. "No matter how far apart we live, we must keep in touch."

"Yes." Isabella nodded. "Always."

The train whistle blew as the two quickly hugged each other.

Isabella broke away with tears in her eyes. "I must go."

"No more sadness now," Lilly said. "Think what an adventure you are going on and how you will be seeing more of America."

"Yes." Isabella nodded and smiled. "It is a

grand adventure. I am ready."

She raised her hand once in goodbye and with Lilly smiling and waving at her, Isabella turned and hurried to board her train.

Once aboard, Isabella found her seat near the window and sat blinking away the rest of her tears with the remnant of a smile on her face. She would miss Lilly. But as Lilly had said, it was now time for her adventure to begin and a new chapter in her life.

As she settled into her seat, she placed the Bible on her lap and looked around the car. Heavy green cloth coverings over the windows would allow them to block the sun if it were too bright. The window coverings matched the seat coverings in a green pattern, which was her favorite color and went well with the dark wooden interior. The seats allowed two to sit together and the car was rapidly filling up.

Men and women and a few small children made up the inhabitants of the train and Isabella found herself enjoying the sight of all the different people in their various hats as they settled in, wondering who would sit beside her and how many of the people would be going all the way to Ohio where she was headed.

A wide-shouldered, bald man who was

holding his hat in his hand sat down beside her.

They nodded at each other and the man said, “Where are you headed, little lady?”

“To Ohio. I’m to meet my fiancé there.” She would establish she had one in case this man was interested in more than polite conversation.

“Ernest Tomlin. At your service.” He placed his hat on the seat beside him and held out his hand.

She placed her gloved hand in his and they shook. “Isabella Britta Stolt.”

“Pleased to meet you, Isabella.”

“Likewise.” She pulled her hand back where he would have held it longer, and placed her hands in her lap, modestly, upon the Bible.

“Where are you from?”

“Sweden.”

“Let me guess. You’re traveling out West. I’ll bet you’re one of those mail order brides.”

Isabella’s jaw dropped. *How did he know?*

He shrugged. “It’s an easy guess. You’re traveling alone and you’re a long way from your home.”

She frowned.

“So you’re headed west to marry a cowboy,” he said. “The great American cowboy women all seem to fall for. It’ll be a harsh life out there. Not like your European cities.”

"I'm not going out West," she said.

"No? Not marrying a cowboy?"

She shook her head no.

"Where are you going, then?"

She pursed her lips. "I'm not going to tell you. I've said too much already."

Opening her Bible to read, she showed the most horrendous of manners by ignoring him completely. Perhaps if she were rude he would leave her alone.

He settled back against the seat but she still felt his gaze upon her.

She read several of her favorite Psalms, the ones that had a way of comforting and calming her.

An older couple sat down across from them with the woman directly across from Isabella and the man across from Mr. Ernest Tomlin.

She felt a bit more comfortable with them there to observe Mr. Tomlin. She nodded at them and then returned to her reading.

The train gave a small lurch and then they were rolling down the tracks, with the rails clicking along beneath them as they rolled away from the station toward Chicago.

Her trip involved changing trains at a few of the stations and this might have been confusing but Mr. Donald Jenks had made sure all her tickets were correct.

Isabella felt she was in good hands. All she had to do was follow the instructions and enjoy the scenery and the company of her fellow travelers.

Though not that of Mr. Ernest Tomlin, who was now looking at her and clearing his throat.

She ignored him and hid deeper inside her silent reading. After about ten minutes, Isabella closed her Bible and stood. The man made her stomach nervous and she needed to eat something now to calm it.

That, and perhaps a cup of tea would put her to rights again.

Moving away from Mr. Tomlin, she headed for the dining car.

In the red and gold car, she took a seat at a table for two by the window. Settling herself, she waited for someone to take her order. Watching as the trees rolled past and feeling the rumble of the train over the tracks beneath her as she sat in the cushioned seat, enjoying the scenery.

The rumble of the wheels over the tracks created a rhythm, which had her thoughts drifting in a most pleasant way as she watched out the window.

Caught up in her restful, dreaming state of

mind, she didn't notice Mr. Tomlin until he sat right across from her.

Goodness, would the man follow me everywhere? Even to the dining car? Is there no break from him? He certainly does talk a lot and ask a lot of questions.

Sitting across from her, he said, "What are you having, tea?"

She nodded but remained silent.

A waiter came to take their order and, assuming they were together, left the ordering to Mr. Tomlin.

He placed an order for sandwiches, cakes, and tea. More than one person could eat. When he waved the man away, she suddenly realized what he was doing.

"Oh but we're not together," she told the waiter who ignored her and, taking the order, moved away without a word.

She frowned. Mr. Tomlin should not be ordering for her. She raised an eyebrow at him. "We are not together," she repeated.

"We are sharing the same table," he said, "and the least I can do, having somehow offended you earlier, is to offer you my apologies and buy you lunch."

Sighing, Isabella said, "You don't have to do that."

"Yes, I do.," he said. "I can't leave it the way things are, with you offended and that silence you're putting off. It's very off putting, you know. I wouldn't advise you use that on your new husband."

Well goodness, it is meant to be off putting. Though it does not seem to be working with you.

"How I behave around him is none of your business." She spoke quiet and low so as not to make a spectacle in front of the other diners. "I do not know you sir, and have no wish to." So saying, she stood and walked away from the table.

Ernest Tomlin watched the quiet blonde leave.

She'd be perfect. The boss would love to get his hands on merchandise like her. Being European meant she had that sexy accent people would pay extra for and there wasn't any family to miss her. Yeah. She could disappear nice and easy.

His partner sat down across from him, in the spot Isabella had just occupied.

Tomlin grimaced at the smell of him. His one redeeming feature was that he had enormous hands like meat hocks that were useful for restraining victims.

"You want that one?"

CHAPTER 3

"You bet I do," Tomlin replied. "If a window pops up on the next stop we can take her there."

"What if she doesn't get off the train?" His partner asked.

"Then we'll just follow her to the end of the line and make arrangements. We've done it before. She's worth doing it again."

The dirty man leaned back in his chair, tipping his hat over his eyes. "Hell, I'd settle for just grabbing that big money bag of hers."

Ernest grunted. "I'll be happy with that, but a piece like her would go a long way towards making friends with the boss. Just be ready."

Hesitantly, Isabella approached the bar at the

back of the dining car and ordered a glass of sweet wine instead of the tea. Leaning with her hands upon the bar she closed her eyes for one brief moment to collect herself.

Ernest Tomlin had driven her to this.

She had completely lost any appetite she'd had and now needed a drink to calm her nerves and still her shaking hands. She'd heard of being driven to drink but this was the first time she had experienced it.

A small glass to settle the nerves, mother would have said.

Mother had pulled out an old bottle of wine, reserved for special occasions, the night before they left on their journey to America and her family and their neighbors had toasted to a safe journey.

A small glass to settle my nerves, which is exactly what I shall do now.

The bartender smiled kindly at her as he gave her the glass.

Isabella smiled back. "Thank you." Sipping it, she made a face.

American wine was very different from the wine in Sweden. This wine was drier, sharper, without the smooth notes from centuries of vineyards and the more refined taste of European wine.

A soft chuckle made her glance sideways. There was a man sitting there trying to stifle his handsome grin.

Seeing he was caught, he said, "I'm sorry. I don't mean to offend. Not used to wine?"

Isabella shook her head. "Not American wine."

"Ah," he said. "I understand. Not from around here, huh?"

"Not from around here." She nodded, taking in his clean-cut appearance from his plain brown suit, to his blonde haircut and shaved chin.

He was, as her mother would have described, well put together and tidy in the way that careful men were.

Mother was always cautioning her about being careful around men and after her last conversation with Mr. Tomlin she'd determined to be more careful with men she did not know.

She had told Mr. Tomlin too much about herself and she could not do that kind of thing again while traveling alone.

Even if there was something about this man which made her feel comfortable in his presence.

Isabella nodded and watched the handsome, careful man, wondering who he was.

The man nodded and stuck out his hand. “I’m Tom.”

She gave him a small smile.

He had nice eyes. Blue and clear, something about them made her want to smile wider.

She reached her hand out to meet his. “Isabella.” And then decided to tell him just a bit more. “From Sweden.”

“Good to meet you, Isabella.” He smiled. “From Sweden.”

His hand lingered in hers, not drawing back right away, as she was used to. His grip was strong, but not tight. It was comfortable and just right. His skin, tan from the sun, was not soft, but it was not calloused either.

She liked his strong hands and his intelligent eyes.

At that moment, a man at the other end of the bar called Tom’s name.

Turning away reluctantly, Tom took his hand back and waved to him.

Returning to Isabella, he nodded. “It was very nice to meet you, Isabella. Welcome to America.”

“Thank you Tom. It was my pleasure,” she said.

The palm of her hand still tingled from where he had touched her and the way he had lingered.

She clasped her hands together, let go a breath she hadn't known she'd held, and watched him go.

Returning to her seat across from the older couple, Isabella was happier than when she'd left, and quite happy to note Mr. Tomlin was no longer seated next to her.

Instead, a thin elderly gentleman with a cane was seated there in his place.

Oh good. Perhaps after our next stop, Mr. Tomlin will not be boarding again.

"Is this seat taken?" she asked the gentleman.

"It wasn't but it is now," he said with a voice so high it almost squeaked. He gestured to the seat. "Please my dear, sit down."

"Thank you," she said. She sat and placed her Bible on her lap.

He noted the Bible and nodded at her in approval.

She relaxed back into her seat. Perhaps she might enjoy this leg of the trip now and be able to watch the scenery outside the window.

"I'm headed to Cincinnati to visit my son," he said. "And spend some time with all my grandchildren."

"Oh that's wonderful. How many do you have?"

"Four in Cincinnati and three back home in Boston."

"That's quite a distance to travel."

"Forgive me my dear, I neglected to properly introduce myself." He stood and gave a slight bow as formal as any she'd ever seen. "Mr. Banning, at your service."

"Isabella Stolt," she would have stood and curtsied if it wouldn't have seemed out of place, but instead she dipped her head. "So very pleased to meet you."

"The pleasure is mine, my dear, believe me." He sat again and they smiled at each other. Then he continued. "To answer your question, it may seem like quite a distance to travel for some. But I don't count the miles because they bring me closer to my family. Though I do wish our youngest son lived closer. He took a job managing a factory in Cincinnati and moved the family there. I would have had him stay closer to home. I cannot visit them more than twice a year."

"Will you be there through the holidays?"

"Yes, I will. I'm looking forward to spending Christmas with the children. John is ten, Elizabeth is eight, Stuart is four and Lucy is just three months old."

"Oh how wonderful. Is this your first time seeing the baby?"

"Yes, it is."

He was such a nice, grandfatherly man that she didn't mind sharing a bit more about herself when he asked, "Where are you traveling to?"

"Yellow Springs, Ohio. This is my first time traveling westward. I have lived in Lawrence, Massachusetts and in New York City."

"This is a pleasant way to travel and the route is scenic."

"Yes, I have been enjoying seeing the towns and the countryside as it flashes by the windows."

"He has been moving us at a pretty good clip today." He nodded. "We'll reach the station a bit early, I believe. You may as well get off the train and stretch your legs a bit," Mr. Banning said. "They'll be loading firewood and coal and be changing engineers and conductors at this stop. There's no reason for you to sit in your seat all that time waiting."

"Oh, thank you for letting me know," she said. "Yes, I believe I shall."

"I'll be off to a little shop I know to purchase a new pipe and tobacco, otherwise I might join you."

"Thank you. I'm sure I shall be fine. It will be nice to be off to stretch my legs. I do love a nice long walk."

"Be careful you don't take such a long walk as to miss your train."

"I shall." She smiled.

The next few miles passed quickly as she enjoyed both the scenery and her new companion's company and then the whistle blew and the train pulled into the station.

Many of the passengers stood to exit the train and Mr. Banning, ever the gentleman, followed her down the aisle and down the steps. At the bottom he said, "Remember now, enjoy your walk but don't tarry too late and miss the train."

She laughed. "Yes, I will remember."

At the train station, people hurried about their business. Steam from the train blew across the walkway and the gray clouds overhead threatened rain. But none of the darkening clouds dampened Isabella's uplifted spirits as she started off on her walk.

Smiling as she walked, passengers, some noting her good mood, smiled and nodded in return and she felt all was right with the world. Passengers hurried past her, but she, enjoying each moment, simply breathed in the air and enjoyed her walk.

Then Isabella was jostled and her father's Bible knocked from her hand.

Oh! Father's Bible.

Everything happened so fast. She bent to pick up the Bible. A white piece of paper had escaped and was blowing away. "Oh, no!"

Father's letter.

The one he'd written to her from him and mother before they passed. Separated from her parents because of the quarantine, these were the last words from her parents.

She'd bookmarked a passage in Psalms with it. She couldn't lose that letter.

The white paper went tumbling and then lifted and tumbled, away from her. She lifted her skirts and gave chase to it. Down around the corner. Dark clouds overhead blocked the sun and the first raindrops began to fall.

The letter, she almost had it. She bent to reach for it, and two men grabbed her.

CHAPTER 4

One man pulled Isabella up and back, a hand around her shoulders and another over her mouth. The other man raced around in front of her, pulling her hands together with one big hand while his other hand pulled out a length of rope. They were pulling her toward an open door in the side of the building.

Isabella gave a muffled scream, but the hand on her mouth was tight. Her eyes, wide and terrified, fixed on the man in front of her, who was wrapping her wrists with rope as they dragged her closer to the dark room. He was grinning at her, and her mind strangely fixated on how unkempt he was. His teeth were yellowed, his nose bent out of place. Long hair fell into his face, shaggy and dirty. He looked up at her and leered, grinning.

They were almost there, now.

Isabella gave one last, terrific heave, but the man behind her was so strong, and the other man laughed, about to tighten a knot. Then Isabella heard a thud, and suddenly the man behind her released her and fell.

Isabella fell to one side, but turned, landing on her shoulder with a painful thud.

She saw another man fighting the dirty one who had tied her wrists. The new man was much cleaner than the first.

He was much faster, too, throwing punches like lightning that landed on the dirty man's face or body. Finally, the new man knocked the other man down, who scrambled backwards as the new man drew a pistol from under his coat and pointed it at him.

Without a word, the dirty man got up and ran away.

For a moment, the clean man looked around, and Isabella was able to study him. It was only then she realized her rescuer was Tom from the dining car.

Apparently satisfied that all was well, Tom put his pistol away and looked down at her, his blue eyes intense and filled with concern. Holding out a hand, he asked, "Are you all right?"

Slowly, she reached her hands up to him, her wrists still bound by the rope, her fingers reaching toward him to accept his hand. "Yes. Thank you."

He pulled her up, by grasping her arms, but it made her dizzy, and the moment he let go of them, she stumbled.

Suddenly she was in his arms, rain falling down all around them, her bound wrists against his chest. Looking into his eyes, as blue as her own, she saw his strength. Her heart racing from the near abduction now skipped and she caught her breath. Sparks fired between them. As the rain covered them with droplets, neither seemed to notice in that brief moment.

And then the moment was gone.

"You're safe now."

"Yes." She breathed the word as her words started to return from the emotional place she had been. The danger, the fright, the sudden attraction to Tom had stolen her words briefly.

He began to untie her hands and her gaze dropped to his hands as she watched.

"Thank you," she spoke again with a shiver, as the rope began to be pulled away. Gratitude filled her. The slight shiver, an aftereffect of nearly being abducted, spread through her, and the chill of the rain contributed to the shaky feeling.

After untying her wrists, Tom gathered her close, rubbing her wrists and then running his hands up and down her arms, warming her and fighting back the chill just as he'd fought back her abductors.

She leaned in close to him resting against his strength as he warmed her. She closed her eyes, breathing in his scent.

Safe.

She was safe now and warming beneath his hands. At that moment, another man came running around the corner and she opened her eyes, startled.

Apparently he was looking for Tom, but he stopped the moment he saw them. "Should I come back later?"

Tom rolled his eyes. "Just stay with him, Bill."

Tom nodded toward the man who'd grabbed Isabella from behind, now lying unconscious on the ground.

The man was Ernest Tomlin.

Isabella gasped.

The man moaned and began to stir.

Taking the hint, Bill walked over and gave him a swift kick in the gut.

Tom turned back to Isabella. "I'm so sorry you had to go through that. Tomlin and his gang have been robbing and snatching women all along this train line for months."

Isabella's eyes grew wide. "Are you a constable?"

Tom smirked. "Something like that."

"Thank you for saving me."

"It was my pleasure."

Their eyes did a connecting dance, rare in any meeting of two souls, but especially rare in a first meeting. That initial fire lit a strong burn of desire.

Caught up in the moment, she forgot she was engaged to Mr. Donald Jenks. But then that reality returned to her and she blinked and, pulling back slightly, looked down with a blush.

"And now," Tom said as she looked up at him again, "Let me see you safely back to the train."

"Yes, please." She nodded feeling suddenly shy and unsure of herself.

He placed her hand in the bend of his arm and he began to escort her back to the train calmly taking charge and behaving like a proper gentleman.

"Hey!" Bill shouted at them, and they turned. "You forget something?" He held up Isabella's

Bible in one hand and her father's letter in the other.

"Father's letter," she said, relief filling her entire body. She rushed back to Bill and took them both with a hurried, "thank you."

Everything would be fine now.

Tom smiled as she walked back to him, after tucking the letter safely inside the Bible. She gazed at Tom with happy tears in her eyes. "I was afraid I'd lost it."

"Glad to see you didn't," he replied. "Those must be very precious to you."

"Oh they are." She blinked up at him. "These are my mother and father's last words to me and this is my family Bible."

"Precious things indeed," Tom said. "My family had a Bible back home, so big I couldn't lift it until I was twelve." He held out his arm again and she placed her hand upon it.

Moving once again toward the train, they rounded the corner.

As they walked, she stopped suddenly, her hand reaching to her side, which was empty. "Oh no."

"What's wrong?" His gaze followed the movement of her hand, as he wondered if she'd been injured by the manhandling.

"My bag. It's gone." She looked at him with those wide blue eyes. "All my money was in it. Now it's gone. All the money Mr. Donald Jenks gave me is gone."

Tom pursed his lips, frustrated with himself. "I bet Tomlin's guy took it."

"My fiancé will not be happy."

"Perhaps not about the money," Tom said, turning back to her. "But he should be happy to know you're safe and unharmed."

"Well I don't know." She looked down. "I don't know him well enough to know."

Looking back up at Tom's face, she watched an expression flash, and then vanish. "Do you still have your tickets?" Concern showed on his face as he asked.

"Oh." She seemed flustered for a moment as she paused and then her face brightened. "Yes. I must still have them. I had placed them in my pocket." She reached her hand into her pocket to touch them and reassure herself they were indeed there. "Yes. I have them."

"Very good." He nodded. "If we find your money, I'll deliver it myself. Where can I find you?"

Isabella gave him the address of Mr. Donald Jenks in Yellow Springs, Ohio.

He made a note of it and then, tucking her hand again in the bend in his arm, he escorted her to the train.

Helping her aboard, they paused, she on the train, he on the platform.

He was about to say something when the conductor shouted "All aboard!"

Not knowing what else to do, Tom quickly kissed the back of her hand just as the train started moving.

She stood watching him as the train rolled away. Raising her gloved hand she waved.

He stood watching her go.

Finally, Isabella turned and found her way back to her seat beside the window, next to Mr. Banning.

"Well, did you enjoy your walk?" he asked.

She sank back into her seat, hardly knowing where to start or how to answer him. She took a deep breath and gave a great sigh.

He took one look at her face and his jovial expression changed to serious. "What happened?"

"I." She started and stopped, remembering what had happened.

Mr. Banning frowned in concern. "Take your time."

"I was walking and out of nowhere some men

grabbed me and they...” She stopped and closed her eyes. *The telling of it was not so easy.*

“Are you injured?” Mr. Banning inquired, his concern for her immediate.

“No, I am fine now.” She opened her eyes and looked at him. “There was another man there. One who saved me.”

Her thoughts were all over, out of sequence, everything she’d felt and seen jumbling together so that she couldn’t tell the story straight through. Her mind was too full and it had all been so recent. Each wonderful and horrible moment.

She gazed out the window.

Tom. Where was he now? Who was he?

“Are you sure you’re all right?” Mr. Banning asked.

“He said he wasn’t a constable, but something like that.” her voice drifted.

Something like that. What did that mean?

“The man who saved you?”

“Yes.” She turned back to look at Mr. Banning, realizing he’d asked her something. “What did you say?”

“It’s all right my dear.” He patted her hand, which lay on her Bible. “Please continue.”

“Those men who grabbed me, they’d tied my wrists, and I think if he hadn’t come when he did I would not be here now. But Tom, he was there. I'm so glad he was there."

"I'm glad too." Mr. Banning smiled.

"They took my purse with all my money."

"But they didn't take you. And you're fine now. You're going to be fine." Mr. Banning's voice and expression emphasized that point and it sunk in.

Yes. I'm going to be fine now.

"Yes. I am."

He waited watching to see if she wished to speak further of it.

Something about the calm elderly man settled her in a way and she began to settle into the rhythm of the train, the assurance that she was indeed going to be fine, thanks to Tom, and those men who had tried to grab her would soon be far away. Every mile the train traveled would take her farther and farther away and soon she would be safe in Yellow Springs, Ohio.

"If you need anything you just ask," Mr. Banning said.

"I am exhausted. I think I may nap for a bit," she said.

"I'll be right here," he said. "You go on and nap."

She laid her head back against the seat, closed

her eyes and let the rhythm of the train lull her to sleep.

~

THE TRAIN PULLED into the station in Yellow Springs, Ohio and came to a halt.

The closer they'd come to her destination, the more Isabella had peered out the window in anticipation, anxious to see what was to be her new home.

Trees and more trees full of the colors of November, though the leaves were falling, had flashed by the window. But now the train had slowed and was stopping so she could take them all in.

Turning to Mr. Banning she smiled. "It was lovely meeting you, Mr. Banning. I hope you enjoy your time with your family."

Mr. Banning smiled back. "It was lovely meeting you, Miss Stolt. Take care of yourself, my dear."

"Yes, thank you. I will." With that she turned away as Mr. Banning stood to move toward the dining car. Isabella caught a glimpse of trees out her window again.

Oh, it would be lovely here in the spring. I love it here already.

Gathering her things, she moved toward the door of the car, wishing she had a mirror to look in to double check her appearance. She glanced down at her dress.

In just minutes I'll be meeting Mr. Donald Jenks. Whatever will he think of me? All rumpled and dirty from the train. Oh, how I need a bath and to put on a clean dress. But there is no hope of that. He'll be waiting here now to take me to the boarding house. Oh, I hope he's not disappointed in me. I had hoped to look more presentable when he first saw me.

And what will he look like? His letter said he was tall and dark. Would he also be handsome?

Nervously, she twisted her glove in her hands before sliding it back on, grasping the handrail, and stepping down.

She'd barely taken the last step when she heard her name called.

"Isabella." His voice was commanding her attention and she looked over.

There he stood.

Mr. Donald Jenks.

Taking long strides, he moved quickly to stand before her.

She looked up and up into dark brown eyes beneath a hat, which made him appear even taller.

My goodness, but he is tall.

"Isabella. I would have known you anywhere," he said, taking off his hat.

"But how?" She glanced about.

But of course. There were no other short Swedish girls wearing their hair in Swedish braids, and it was a small train station in a small village in the country. Why, there were hardly any other passengers exiting the train. Eight at the most. Of course he'd had no trouble picking her out.

Mr. Jenks smiled at her, his teeth flashing a brilliant white. "I would know you anywhere, my sweet. You are lovelier than I imagined." He took her hand and, giving a deep gentleman's bow, kissed the back of it.

She blushed beneath his flattery and his kiss and was momentarily tongue-tied. For an instant, she was back home, where this sort of thing was commonplace, and it shook her.

"Thank you," she said softly.

He straightened up. "I trust your trip went well."

She froze, and a slight frown crossed her face. *How do I tell him? This man I hardly know who will be my husband. How do I tell him the money he sent me was stolen from me?*

Seeing her distress, he was suddenly serious. "What is it, my dear?"

She swallowed. "Well, I- I did run into some trouble at the station. Two men tried to grab me."

His hands grasped hers and pulled her closer. "I am so glad they did not succeed."

"I was lucky a man was there and stopped them."

Mr. Jenks squeezed her hands and smiled.

My goodness, but he is handsome.

"But someone stole my bag with all the money."

A flash of anger showed in his eyes. Tom's words came back to her.

He should be happy you're safe and unharmed.

But then that flash was gone, or perhaps she had imagined it, for he was now smiling down at her again.

"The main thing is you are here now, safe and sound. I can always make more money." He winked at her. "But you. You, my dear, are more valuable to me than a purse full of money."

He paused, taking her hand again and kissing the back of it, though without his deep bow. Somehow, it made this one seem more intimate. "You are irreplaceable."

"Oh thank you." Relief flooded through her and her words rushed out.

Why, he spoke as if money grew on trees and he'd just go out and get some more. How strange for an accountant. What a funny sort of accountant he is. Oh, I'm so glad he's not a stingy one or one who values money over people.

"I am so glad you feel that way," she said.

"But of course," he said. "You are to be my bride. Wouldn't I treasure my new bride?"

All this time, his eyes had never once broken contact with hers.

She blushed. "I am glad you do." She smiled happily.

Tom was right about Mr. Donald Jenks. He doesn't seem upset about the money. He's just happy to know I am safe and unharmed.

"Now, let's get you over to the resort and settled in," he said. "I'm sure you'll want to freshen up and rest after your long journey. Then I'll take you to dinner and show you some of the town."

"A resort? My goodness. I thought I would be in a small boarding house."

Putting his hat back on, he turned and set her

hand in the bend of his elbow, just as Tom had done.

"Only the best for you, my dear. The Neff House Park Summer Resort is quite popular. And that is where I am taking you to dinner."

"Oh, that sounds lovely! I had no idea there was a resort here."

Though now, I think it makes perfect sense. This is such beautiful countryside!

"Yes," he said, walking easily forward. "People come for the healing water of the springs and to relax. There are many nature trails here in Yellow Springs."

"Oh, I cannot wait to see them." It was at that moment Isabella realized that, though he was so much taller, she was keeping up with him. When she paid attention, she noticed that he was shortening his stride.

How pleasant it is to walk with him.

"Then we shall put that on our list of things to do soon," he said.

At the Neff House, Mr. Jenks saw that her trunks were carried upstairs and that she was settled in her room and a hot bath ordered. Then with a tip of his hat he said, "I shall see you downstairs in two hours for dinner. That should be sufficient time to freshen and rest after your trip."

"Yes," she smiled up at him. "That is perfect."

He kissed the back of her hand again and then turned to leave.

She stood watching him go.

What a handsome man he is. It's a wonder he's not married already. I cannot imagine why such a handsome gentleman would need to advertise for a bride. Any girl would be lucky to be his wife.

She opened her trunk; pulling out the dress she'd wear to dinner tonight and then went to enjoy her bath. A long hot soak was just the thing she needed, along with a fresh change of clothes.

After her bath, Isabella pulled her mother's wedding dress from the trunk and laid it across the bed before smoothing it down with her hands.

The gown was simple but elegant, cream colored with Swedish lace made by her grandmother, who was an excellent hand at tatting.

Mother had looked beautiful in the gown. Also in the trunk was a sketch her father had made of her mother wearing the gown. Isabella pulled the sketch out and looked at it briefly before placing it back amongst her treasures. She didn't know the story behind the sketch, but the love her father felt toward her mother was evident within the lines.

Oh, how I wish for a love like that. For a marriage

which would be a blessing to last all time even up to heaven.

She blinked back a few tears and then smiled, imagining her parents together, smiling, looking down on her, giving her their blessing on her upcoming marriage. If all went well, she'd soon be married and settled down in this charming village with a house and even a garden.

Slipping the dress on she looked into the mirror. The gown fit perfectly and gave her comfort. She ran her hands down the side of her hips and moved from side to side, smiling, watching herself in the mirror as the dress swished and moved with her.

Ever since she was a small girl she had dreamed of the wedding she would someday have. She would be wearing this dress and her handsome groom would gaze into her eyes as if she were the most beautiful creature in the world.

Could her childhood dream possibly be coming true?

Mr. Donald Jenks was so handsome, so tall and just having him look at her made her feel all aflutter.

Slipping out of the gown, she placed it on the bed and prepared to meet Donald for dinner.

Though he'd given her two hours, the time

went by quickly, and soon she was hurrying to dress again. She mustn't be late to meet him.

He seemed like a punctual and precise man, which of course made sense with him being an accountant.

He stood waiting for her at the bottom of the stairs. True to his apparent nature, he was looking at his pocket watch. As he snapped it shut, he looked up and locked eyes with her. Smiling, he said, "You look lovely."

"Thank you," she said.

He offered his arm. "Shall we?"

"Yes." She placed her hand in the bend of his arm and they went to the dining room.

The resort was busier than she would have expected in November and the dining room was full of diners and the tinkle of silverware, plates and glasses. She looked about, taking it all in.

"The food here is very good," he said. "I'm sure you will enjoy it."

"I'm sure I shall."

He held out her chair and she sat.

Their waiter handed them both menus. "May I order for you?" Donald asked.

Surprised, Isabella looked up at him. "Why yes, I suppose."

He gave a brisk nod and then turning to the

waiter said, "The lady will have the lettuce salad, the baked trout with fine herbs, rice croquettes, asparagus tips, and for dessert we will view your selection of pies."

"Very good sir." The waiter gave a nod. "And for you?"

"Consommé of game, the fillet of beef, braised potatoes, peas, and a dish of your salted almonds while we wait. Also, send the wine steward over."

"Excellent." The waiter turned and went to the kitchen.

"I do hope you like fish."

Isabella smiled. "We Swedes eat quite a bit of fish. You might not care for some of them."

"Oh, yes? Why is that?"

"Lutfisk is an acquired taste." She spread her napkin across her lap and smoothed it with her hands. "It's made with white fish such as cod and lye. The fish is soaked for five or six days and becomes gelatinous. Of course before it's served it is soaked in cold water another five days and is quite safe to eat."

Mr. Jenks gave a sigh. "I believe I'll pass on that one."

She laughed. "I thought you might. But it is safe to eat. Truly it is."

"I'll take your word for it, and then," he

winked, “Because you like it, I shall give my portion to you.”

Just then, the wine steward arrived. “Good evening sir.” He handed Mr. Jenks the wine menu.

“Good evening.” He took the menu, gave a brief glance, and ordered the house wine.

“Very good sir,” the steward replied. After he left, Mr. Jenks turned back to Isabella.

She grinned, her eyes flashing. “Now surstromming, that is Swedish for sour herring. It is simply soaked in salt, but it is soaked for six months and develops a smell.”

He chuckled.

“You may find our trout rather plain after such delicacies as you are accustomed to.”

“Oh I am sure it shall be delicious.” She grinned again. “I confess I was sharing the ones which are the most difficult for those who are not Swedish to become accustomed to.”

“Trying to scare me off, are you?”

“Oh no.” Her eyes widened. “Not at all.”

“Good. Because it won’t work.” He placed his hand over hers. “I am smitten.” Her entire face heated as she felt other diners watching them.

“Well,” she said softly. “I shall promise to only serve a dish to you once and if you do not care for it then I shan’t offer it again.”

Before he could reply, the first dishes arrived, with the wine. He squeezed her hand and let go. Picking up his fork he said, “I’ve hired a woman to act as housekeeper and cook for the first month as you settle in, so you’d needn’t worry about what to serve me.”

Well my goodness, she thought. *I won’t have anything to do if someone else is doing all the cooking and the cleaning. Gardening perhaps, but we’re moving into winter. Not the season for gardening.*

“How thoughtful of you,” she said. “But you needn’t do that. I can do all those things.”

With a wave of his hand, he said, “I already brought her in, to get the house ready for you.” He spoke as if that was the final end of it.

Isabella leaned back in her chair, not used to such a tone. Her father had been a man who discussed everything, explaining it to her rather than simply announcing it. The decision to come to America had been discussed for months. She took a sip of wine.

“I might have preferred helping you select the staff,” she said tentatively in a soft voice.

He watched her for a moment and then smiled.

“My dear, I understand. You’ve been fending

for yourself since setting foot in America. But now you can relax and leave everything to me."

Relax and leave everything to him. That does sound good. A part of her relaxed into her chair at the thought.

"My wife shall have the best of everything I can offer her," he continued with a flourish. "I have also engaged a young woman to act as lady's maid the day of our wedding, if you should say yes." He smiled.

There seems to be no reason not to say yes, but I just arrived.

"I have only just arrived," she voiced half of her thoughts, keeping the rest to herself.

"Yes and I understand this is not the time to ask you. It isn't easy, but I will be patient." He pointed to her plate. "How is the trout?"

"Oh very good." She picked up her fork again. "Everything is delicious. You chose well."

"I always do, my dear. In time you will learn to trust me and my decisions."

After dinner, Mr. Jenks said, "Would you like to see the house in the morning? The home, which will be yours, if you accept my marriage proposal?"

She sat up straighter, excited. "Oh, yes, I would. I'd very much like to see it."

He nodded. "Very good. We shall make an early start, after breakfast and then after I show you the house, we shall drive to Springfield and I will show you the company I work for."

"Why do you live so far from where you work?"

Leaning back, he replied, "The country air and peace and quiet of course. I like a quiet home, not one filled with visitors constantly coming and going. I was pleased to learn you too would enjoy quiet country living. A wife who wished to entertain constantly would not be the right wife for me."

"Oh I've no wish to entertain constantly. Though I do like to have friends visit for tea."

"Of course, my dear, of course. After the honeymoon you may have as many people over as you like, for tea or whatever else your heart desires. Until then, I want you all to myself."

She blushed deeply.

He wants me all to himself. Oh my.

Looking up beneath lowered lashes she said, "I'm fine with just you and me for now."

"Very good." He leaned in and said, "You blush so prettily. I must see that you do that often."

She blushed even more. "Well, I... You do seem to bring it out in me."

"Good." He winked. Then he placed his napkin

on the table. “Shall we go for a short stroll? Or do you wish to go back to your room? I don’t want to overtire you.”

“I would love a walk tomorrow. I confess this wonderful dinner and the wine has me full and relaxed tonight. I’m looking forward to a good bed in a room, which doesn’t rock. The train was enjoyable but it’s nice to have ground beneath my feet which isn’t moving.”

“Very well then.” He nodded. “I’ll escort you to your room.”

At the door, the key didn’t work well in the lock, so Mr. Jenks said, “Here. Allow me.” He took the key from her and, with a strong turn, opened the door. Then, swinging it open, he glanced inside the room. Seeing the wedding dress on the bed he appeared surprised.

Seeing his expression, Isabella said, “I was just smoothing out my mother’s wedding dress. Making sure everything was all right. But,” she stepped in front of him in an attempt to block his view. “It’s bad luck to see the wedding dress before the wedding and I want to surprise you.”

He looked over her head toward the dress and frowned. “I’m not fond of surprises.” He stepped inside, ignoring her wish for him to wait to see the dress, and moved over to the bed as she followed him. “No.” He shook his head. “This won’t do. The dress is too plain and old fashioned. And it has yellowed. What would people think?”

Isabella stopped, stunned and hurt by his words. Then she spoke. “It isn’t yellowed. It has always been this cream colored. I’ve taken good care of it.”

Could he not see the beauty in the dress or understand how much it would mean to me to wear it?

Mr. Jenks continued. “I have a position to maintain. I won’t have my bride wearing an old, borrowed dress.”

Isabella stood very still, unsure about the way things were now going.

Everything had been going so well, until now. What if we are not compatible?

CHAPTER 5

Mr. Jenks smiled and warmth came back into his voice. "I see we've already had our first lover's quarrel." He reached for her hands. "You appear distraught, darling. It's only a dress. I'll take you to Madame Boulange's Shop in Springfield and buy you a proper gown."

Isabella, torn by her desire to wear her mother's wedding dress and her wish to please her future husband, gave him her hands, but furrowed her brow.

A proper gown.

"I'll buy you any number of dresses, as many dresses as you want, but please, for me, just this once, allow me to adorn you like the beautiful and elegant woman you are, so that I might show you off to all my friends and business associates."

His business associates. His position. Oh. He wanted a society wedding and I had imagined a little country wedding. Of course he has his position to consider.

She looked into his eyes, which were beseeching her, while his hands gently rubbed hers.

"I, I suppose..." she took a breath and then said, "I shall sleep on it. We've much to discuss before there can be a wedding."

"But of course, my darling." He kissed the back of her hand. "Sleep well then until the morrow. I'll see you again at breakfast."

"Yes. Thank you... Donald."

He gave her a deep smile. "That's what I like to hear."

She walked him to the door. "Good night."

"Good night, my sweet."

She closed the door and moved over to the window, to watch for him to come out of the building. Tired but restless, she wished she were more familiar with the town, enough so that she could go for a walk to clear her head.

Their first lover's quarrel. Yes, she supposed it was, though it was more of a disagreement than a quarrel. She'd merely explained that the dress was not yellowed.

It hadn't felt quarrelsome to her; she'd only been trying to explain about the dress to him.

Isabella wasn't one for raising her voice or getting angry.

As father said, there was no need for shouting, as it didn't make one's argument any more valid simply by raising the volume in the room. Theirs had been a peaceful household given to books and quiet discussion.

I'm glad Donald is not the sort to raise his voice. If this is how we shall quarrel, then we shall have a peaceable house.

She smiled at the thought as she watched him emerge from the building and walk down the sidewalk. He was a tall man with a long stride and made a handsome figure.

What a handsome man he is and how lucky I am to be marrying a man with a good position to maintain.

She glanced down at her dress, realizing though it was fashionable, it was last year's fashion and was a bit worn like most of her dresses. Though he'd not said a word about it, she knew she didn't cut such a fine figure as he. There'd been no time to sew new dresses before boarding the train, nor time to buy one. She wished she had a sewing machine here. Several of the women in Lawrence had shared a machine but that was all behind her now.

I shall have to ask him for a machine after we are married and set about at once to create a new wardrobe fitting my new place in society. I must do all I can as I take my place by his side, to be a wife he can be proud of.

~

THE NEXT MORNING she put on her best dress and took extra time to braid her hair before going downstairs to meet Donald for breakfast.

"Right on time," he said nodding with a smile. "I trust you slept well?"

He seemed so pleased with her punctuality that she made a mental note of this being one way to please him.

"Yes," she smiled in return. "Indeed I did. On a nice soft bed with nothing moving. I feel much better now."

"Very good." He nodded, offered his arm and they headed for the dining room.

She accepted the seat he pulled out for her as the waiter came over with the menus. She hoped

Donald didn't try to order for her this morning. So strong was the thought that when the waiter arrived, she didn't even wait for him to speak.

"I believe I shall have the eggs benedict and orange juice."

There was a flash of surprise from Donald, but he recovered quickly. "And I'll have the same. With tomato juice instead." Without a word, the waiter bowed, tucked the menus under his arm and left.

Donald turned to her and smiled. "I see we share a favorite breakfast."

Isabella gave a slight shrug. "I don't know how to cook the dish, so it is quite a treat for me."

Donald threw back his head and gave a laugh. "Ha! Then I'll have the cook prepare it for you as often as you wish."

She smiled in return, and then cautiously began to speak of thoughts, which had been on her mind. "Mr. Jenks, there are many things we must discuss if we are to be married."

Sensing a shift into a more businesslike mood, Donald sat forward. "Yes, my dear, of course. What would you like to discuss first?"

"Well, you handling everything. I realize a man such as yourself is used to handling every aspect of his life and as you have never been married, you may not realize some wives prefer their husbands leave the handling of certain things to them."

"Please go on," he said. "What would you prefer I let you handle?"

"Well, for one, the hiring of the household servants. A wife would like to be included in this decision-making. To be consulted, and I would hope we would agree on who to hire."

"And if we did not? Then who would decide?"

She blinked. "Why...I don't know. I suppose if it were a cook then I would. If it were a butler you would. Of course I would wish to hire my own lady's maid."

"Oho, and I'd have no say in her hiring I suppose," Donald said with a wag of his finger. "Now that hardly seems fair." Sitting back, he allowed the waiter to serve their breakfast.

"Oh, well it is not. You are right." She said after the waiter had left, picking up her fork. "But no, it would be fair if you were to hire your own valet."

"Indeed." Turning, he signaled for coffee. "And what other reservations do you have, before you would consider me as a husband?"

"Well, you mustn't," she blushed. "You mustn't play patty fingers with any other ladies and must never touch the female servants."

"Of course not." He appeared affronted.

"Whatever would make you think I would do a thing like that?"

"Well. You said you have been single a long time. And I have worked in a house with servants and heard all sorts of tales." She shook her head. "The women can't complain or they would lose their jobs and the men, they take advantage of the younger women. It isn't right."

"You weren't molested by your employer." His words were a question, which made his eyes burn fierce. "You are still a virgin."

"Yes. Yes, I am," she said blushing. "It wasn't me, or my employers. It was a young woman who'd come from another house, serving them and she'd been pursued in a bad way. She nearly took her life. The man wouldn't leave her alone and his wife hated her."

"She finally left them and took a job as helper to the Peterson's cook whose hands were more and more crippled. She'll be happy there. But she told me so many stories of things she and other girls had experienced. It was dreadful."

"And hardly a subject for a fine lady such as you are, or for breakfast." Reaching over, he threaded his fingers through hers, holding her hand on the table. "My dear Isabella. I have never behaved as less than a gentleman toward any lady.

It is my great hope that in time you'll forget the sordid things of your past. Toiling in the factory, working as a servant. All those things you experienced and the stories you heard. It's time to set those things aside and move into a better life. One that I can give you. Allow me to show you the house after we eat and then you can make your decision with all of the facts of what I have to offer you."

Isabella brightened at the thought. "I would love to see the house."

"Very good." Donald leaned back, returning his thoughts briefly to breakfast. "Now as to the question of church. As you know, there's no Lutheran church in town. There is a United Methodist church and we're more than welcome to marry there if we choose to. I've already spoken to the pastor."

"My goodness. You have been busy," she said, arching her eyebrow.

"There are many details to attend to if there's to be a wedding. Which is yet to be determined. Are you ready for that walk now?"

"Yes and I cannot wait to see the house." Isabella put down her fork and placed her napkin on the table.

He stood and held out his hand to her. She

took it and rose. Then with his hand on the small of her back, he guided her through the dining room.

Outside Neff House, they stood on the long porch and he pointed down the street. “My house is on Jackson Street, just a few blocks to the north, on the edge of town.”

“I do love to go for walks,” she said. “It’s something I used to do every day, back in my homeland. When I worked at the factory I was too tired to go walking after I got off and with the Petersons I had to stay there and sing the children to sleep before I could go home, so there was no time.”

Donald smiled. “Now that you’re here you must take all the walks you wish.”

“I believe I shall.” As they rounded a corner, Isabella gasped. The house was everything she’d dreamed of and more. A walkway bordered by yellow rose bushes led to a white two-story house with a large front porch.

“Oh how lovely,” she said. A smile of wonder crossed her face.

It really was happening. A dream house and a husband to be, who was more handsome and charming than she could’ve imagined. It felt like stepping into a beautiful dream. Far better than her daydreams had been.

After a long moment, Donald leaned close, whispering, "Would you prefer to see the house first or the garden?"

"Oh." She clasped her hands together and gazed brightly into his eyes. "The garden."

"I thought as much," he nodded with a chuckle.

She smiled up at him.

"Come." He placed her hand on his arm and led her around the house to the back to where the garden was.

"Oh." She stopped short at the sight, which awaited her and she caught her breath. Rows of flowers met her gaze. Tall orange ones, medium yellow ones and smaller red ones. The tall orange ones waved in the wind as if saying hello and yellow rose bushes were planted on each side of the garden. A birdbath adorned by cherubs stood in the middle, with rows spreading out around the circular middle like spokes on a wagon wheel. The garden was orderly, yet overgrown as if the flowers had tried to take over, escaping their boundaries. Never had she seen such a profusion of cheerful color in a garden, with yellow predominating.

"They're lovely." She turned a beaming face up at him, "and so cheerful. Why, you can't help but smile and be happy when you look at them. I simply love them, Donald. This garden is perfect. Far beyond what I'd dreamed of."

"As are you." He bent down on one knee.

She caught her breath and held it as he reached inside his pocket for a ring.

Gazing into her eyes said, "Isabella Britta Stolt, will you do me the honor of marrying me?"

CHAPTER 6

Isabella let her breath out and said, "Yes."

The gold ring, in the shape of a leaf, held a ruby in the center, with a ring of rose cut diamonds around it. Donald slid the ring onto her finger and she gazed down at it in awe.

This really is happening.

The house, the handsome husband and this beautiful ring.

It felt as if she'd stepped into one of the fairy tales she'd read as a child. All the bad things, which had happened to her since coming to America, had brought her to this moment. The beginning of her happy ever after.

"It's beautiful," she said as she gazed at the ring, which caught the light in the facets of the stones making it appear even lovelier. She turned her hand this way and that.

"I'm glad it pleases you." Rising, Donald brought her near and bent down, wrapping his arms softly around her waist.

Isabella's hands gently landed on his strong chest and she gazed up into his eyes. They closed as his lips descended.

His lips brushed hers softly at first. Caught in the emotion of the moment, she let herself give in. The sensations, all so new, swept her away as her eyes closed, her breath caught and she kissed him back instinctively.

When he broke away, Donald stood looking down on her and said, "You have made me the happiest of men."

Beaming up at him she said, "I am happy too."

"I'm glad. Now, shall I show you the inside of the house?"

"Oh," she said, remembering that she hadn't yet seen it. "Yes, please."

Placing her hand in the bend of his arm he led her to the house.

In the parlor was a fireplace. "Oh, it's perfect," she said.

"I'm pleased that you like it."

Everywhere she looked the furniture was polished, as were the wooden floors in the parlor and the dining room. The house had, as he'd said, been readied for a new bride. Yellow and gold were throughout the house in the draperies, the upholstery and the carpets. It gave a cheerful mood to the dark somber wood and the contrast was one Isabella found charming.

She walked about, touching the furniture and looking. "So lovely," she said, looking up at him. "And cheerful."

"And all yours," Donald said with a smile. "I'm glad you find it cheerful."

"Is yellow your favorite color?" she asked.

"No," he shook his head. "I prefer red. Come let me show you the kitchen."

"Yes, and I would like to meet our cook."

"Mrs. Blevins isn't in today. She'll return the day of our wedding. As will Dolcinda, your lady's maid for the day. There's time enough to meet them later. Today we have the house to ourselves."

Upstairs were three bedrooms. The largest had a window, which overlooked the garden in the back. She walked to the window and looked out. A red bird landed on the limb of a large oak tree near the window.

Donald followed her over to the window. "This will of course be our room."

"It has a lovely view," she said, still watching the bird.

"That's a cardinal," he said as he slipped his arm around her waist. "Does the house suit you? You may redecorate it as you see fit."

"Oh yes, it does." She looked up at him "I shall be very happy here, with things just as they are."

I'm pleased to hear it," he said. "We'll keep things as they are." He took her hand and led her away from the window. "We've much to do before the wedding. We'll go into Springfield today and pick out your dress."

"Oh, today?" Surprise filled her voice.

"Yes. We must get things started without delay. Come, I'll take you back to your room to freshen up and then we must be off."

Everything is happening so fast all at once. Today I've had my first kiss and become engaged! And now we must shop for my wedding gown. Right away.

"Everything is happening so quickly."

"We've a lot to do to get ready for the wedding. There are many details to attend to."

"Yes, of course there are."

Back in her room, she took a minute to catch her breath.

Mr. Jenks was so enthusiastic about their wedding and so full of plans that his enthusiasm wore her out.

We must shop for the wedding dress today, for Mr. Jenks insists. He's so eager to marry. Why, I only just arrived yesterday and have barely had a chance to catch my breath.

Donald was taking charge of everything, every last detail of the wedding, with a speed, which was astonishing.

He's so busy making these plans and so excited to be married. Such enthusiasm to be wed. I've never seen the like in a man.

Yesterday I arrived, today I am engaged, and now we go to shop for my dress. Tomorrow I have only a few hours to myself to rest and we will pick up my dress. The following day we will be married. So soon!

Three days after she stepped off the train, she would become Mrs. Donald Jenks.

Mr. Donald Jenks was adamant about her need for a grand wedding gown. One befitting his position in society. She pushed aside the hurt that lingered from his dismissal of her mother's gown as plain and old fashioned.

Of course I must take my place beside him in society. That is the way things are done.

Placing the gown away in the trunk, she then closed the lid more heavily than she'd intended and tried not to think of the heavy feeling on her heart. He would call upstairs for her soon, once the carriage was ready to drive her into town where they would go shopping.

I must put away the past and move into the future. My future now is pleasing my husband and making a new and happy life here.

She moved over to the window to look out. In the distance, a train was leaving the station. She could see the column of steam from the stack of the engine.

Her thoughts drifted to Tom.

Where was Tom now and what was he doing? Has he given any thought to me since we met or has he forgotten all about me? It was too bad he couldn't be here in town. I would invite him to the wedding. It would be nice to have at least one friend near.

He had such a calm comforting presence, which might have calmed her nervousness about this wedding.

Madame Boulange's shop in Springfield, Ohio was full of the latest wedding fashions.

Isabella stood inside the door, holding on to Donald's arm and looking about. More wedding gowns than she'd ever seen filled the room and all in unfamiliar styles.

"This is the latest design from France," Madame Boulange assured Mr. Donald Jenks, holding up a dress with huge puffed sleeves. "These are the best quality."

He looked the dress over as she turned it from front to back, with her assistant displaying the long train. He nodded his approval.

"And the veil."

With astonishment, Isabella realized the veil was as long as the train. "It's so long."

"Yes," Madame Boulange nodded. "With Queen Victoria's wedding all the gowns changed. Brides must wear white, for purity, and a longer veil." Isabella frowned, thinking of the soft cream-colored gown, which had been her mother's.

No wonder Mr. Donald Jenks didn't want me wearing mother's dress and thought it had yellowed. As a virgin I must wear white. How embarrassed I would've been had I worn the dress and not understood the customs in America. Everything is so different here and I must do all I can to adapt to my new country.

Somehow now mother's gown didn't seem as lovely, as if Madame Boulange and Mr. Jenks had sullied it somehow. Sadness filled her heart.

But weddings were supposed to be joyous occasions.

Not wishing to appear an ignorant country bumpkin, Isabella resigned herself to wearing whatever Madame Boulange recommended and resolved to think only happy thoughts about it.

Donald stepped into the other room to wait as Isabella tried the dress on.

The gown, after its massive cloth was slipped over her head and onto her arms, felt heavy. The material was thick and covered with decorative trims, which hung heavy upon her small frame. She felt lost inside of it, like a small doll.

Madame Boulange bustled about, pulling here and there. "The sleeves are too long and the hem must be taken up or she will trip." She snapped her fingers and her assistant came with the pins.

Taking one pin after another the assistant adjusted the gown so it could be taken in.

After removing the dress, Isabella stood in her underclothes with goose bumps on her arms, chilled, but relieved the heavy dress had been removed.

Madame then fitted her with underclothes, which included white silk stockings with embroidery running down the entire front.

When all the underclothes had then been

taken away, and when Isabella was once again clothed in her day gown, Madame Boulange said, “The gentleman may return,” in such a voice she might have been announcing royalty.

Mr. Donald Jenks stepped back into the room. Turning her attention to him, Madame Boulange said, “I can have the fitting completed by tomorrow evening at the earliest.”

“I’ll pay extra for your quickest work as we discussed. We marry the day after tomorrow.” I don’t wish to wait one hour longer than necessary to be wedded to my beautiful bride.” He gave Isabella a smoldering look that made her feel aflutter.

He was so handsome, and that look. Oh my. What a lucky girl I am to be marrying such a handsome man.

“Now gloves,” Madame spoke breaking the moment. “Let me see your hands.”

Isabella held them out.

“These will fit I believe.”

Isabella took the white kid gloves and slid them on. They did fit perfectly but were the strangest gloves she’d ever seen. There was a slit near her ring finger. She pointed to it. “Madame, I do not understand this opening.”

“For the ring of course.”

“I see.”

How perfectly impractical. Such gloves would be for a one-time use only.

"My bride hasn't lived in the city. She's less familiar with the latest fashions," Donald explained.

It sounded as if he was apologizing for her ignorance and once again she was embarrassed and feeling like a country bumpkin.

"Not to worry her sweet head about it," Madame spoke to him as if Isabella were not standing right there. "This is of course why you come to me. When I am finished with her, none will be able to tell. Now your slippers." Madame pointed to Isabella's feet. "We must take the measure of your feet."

Her assistant brought a chair and placed it behind Isabella. Taking a measuring instrument, the assistant measured one foot, and then the other. Then she stood and whispered into Madame's ear.

Madame nodded.

The assistant went into the back room and returned carrying a pair of white kid slippers with a one-inch heel. The perfect height for a genteel young lady.

She placed the slippers upon Isabella's feet and they fit perfectly. "Just so," the assistant said and nodded, satisfied.

Isabella stood and walked in the slippers. "Yes, they fit fine," she said.

"Now your initials are?" Madame Boulange asked.

"I. B. S., Isabella Britta Stolt," Isabella said.

"A lovely name," Madame Boulange said, but with such an air of boredom it felt to Isabella as if she said that to every bride. "Now select your handkerchief trim color."

"Green. It is my favorite color."

"She will have red," Mr., Donald Jenks interrupted. "That is my favorite color."

Madame nodded and wrote that down. "Red it is." She looked up again. "We are complete."

Isabella breathed a sigh of relief. All the trying on and fitting and selecting of things was done. She'd never been more tired after a day of shopping in her life. All she wanted now was to be back at the Neff House where she could slip into her warm soft nightgown and curl beneath the blankets and sleep.

They exited Madame Boulange's shop and Donald said, "We'll drive past the Altschul Distilling Company before we head back to Yellow Springs and I will show you the distillery I work for."

I would love to see it," Isabella said. "You

haven't said much about your work. What does your company distill?"

"Whiskeys, bourbon, rye, gin, brandy and wine."

"My goodness that's quite a selection for one distillery." She laughed. "I only drink wine."

"You must tell me the type of wine you like so I can order it in for you. Was there any particular kind you'd like to have for our wedding?"

"Just champagne, for the toasts."

Donald nodded. "Very good."

"Do you commute to Springfield every day for work?"

"The distillery I'm going to show you is in Springfield, but the offices are in Dayton, which is in the other direction."

"Oh I see. So your home in Yellow Springs is in the middle, which makes it easier for you when you have to commute both places."

"Yes, my home in Yellow Springs is making everything much easier." Donald smiled a deep smile, almost as if he were having a thought he wasn't sharing with her.

Whatever can he be thinking?

But then his eyes lit up as he turned to look on her and he said, "I used to keep a townhome, but was drawn to a country home just as your dream was to live in one, so now I'll only go into the office when I need to."

"I see. I had wondered with your work, how often you'd be home."

"You mustn't worry that I'll be leaving you so soon. I can bring the account books home to work on them there. And I've arranged to do that for a while as we're settling into married life. So you shall have my company all day and all evening, though I may be in at my desk working."

"How generous of your employers to allow that."

"As I said, I have a position to maintain and I'm well respected among the management of the company. And now, here we are." They'd pulled up in front of the brick building and sat looking at it. "This is where any shipments to our house would come from. I'm not here often as I handle the accounts from the offices in Dayton, but we do audits twice a year at this facility."

Isabella nodded as she watched shipments being loaded to go out in large wagons. "It's a busy place."

"Yes it is. Now if you'll wait here, I will go in and place an order for our wedding reception."

"Yes, of course."

Donald went into the building and she sat

waiting, wondering exactly what he had planned for the reception. Things were moving so fast and he had it all in hand, but she did wish she knew more what was going on as far as his plans.

It's obvious he's not used to consulting or informing anyone about his decisions. He's been a single man for so long. I must be patient with him.

When Donald returned, they began to travel back to Yellow Springs. "I'll show you Dayton another time. And you'll meet many of my business associates at the wedding reception."

"I will look forward to both," she said, "And I'm glad you have a good job in such thriving cities as Springfield and Dayton, but I'm also glad we are to live in Yellow Springs. I'm not so much a city girl."

"I gathered as much from your letters."

"Still, it's a nice city and I like that there are so many trees here. It makes a place feel more welcoming when there are trees."

"Indeed it does my dear and I'm glad you feel welcome here." Donald winked. "I knew you would and just wait until I show you the walking paths near our house. You'll love them I'm sure of it."

"It sounds lovely."

~

When Donald came to pick her up and take her to Springfield to collect her finished dress, he said, "I have a surprise for you."

"Oh," her eyes lit up. "Thank you."

Proudly, he handed her a new leather Bible with gilt lettering.

She held it for a moment, looking at the beautiful Bible and then said, "Well this is a lovely Bible, really it is, but I was already planning to carry father's Bible since he's not here to walk me down the aisle."

"Isabella." Donald's tone rebuked her. "Whatever can you be thinking? That worn out old Bible isn't suitable for our wedding. What would our new friends and neighbors think?"

The old, cracked leather showed signs of wear and the gold of the gilt lettering had worn off in many places. Still, the Bible had great value and meaning to her and in her eyes it was beautiful.

He shook his head. "No. You weren't thinking again. This one will replace it."

At her continued look of reluctance, Donald appeared hurt by her rejection of the gift. "I thought..." He spoke quietly and paused. "You might read a verse or two from it in the evenings."

Oh the poor man. I've hurt his feelings. He doesn't

even attend church and he's given me this Bible, which he wants me to read to him. Oh how can I ever say no.

"Oh. Yes, of course. I'd be happy to."

"Thank you." His facial expression relaxed into the pleasant one she liked so much.

He's done nothing but try to give me nice things he thinks I might want or need. I mustn't appear so ungrateful for all he's done and is trying to do. He's trying, so I must try too.

"It is I who should thank you. It is lovely and I will treasure your gift. Thank you."

"You're quite welcome my dear. I only wish to make you happy. Now let's go and collect your dress."

CHAPTER 7

They drove back to Springfield to pick up her dress.

Madame Boulange, pleased with her work, announced that Isabella was one of the loveliest brides she'd ever seen.

Isabella suspected Madame said the same thing to every bride to be.

There was, of course, the secrecy of not letting Donald see his bride in her gown. Soon it was packed and they were on their way back to Yellow Springs.

On the way Donald explained who each of the guests invited to the wedding were, as Isabella tried to make mental notes of so that she didn't commit any faux pas, which would affect his position. From the way he spoke, he must have a very important job.

~

Tomorrow I shall be married. Oh, how I wish Lilly could be here. There isn't one person I know who will be at our wedding. Not one friend or person I know other than Donald.

She moved to the window to look out and thought of Lilly, wondering how she was.

I promised to write to her, to let her know I arrived safely. Everything has happened so fast there's been little time. Donald hasn't even given me a full week to prepare myself for the wedding. How anxious he is to marry me.

In time surely we'll grow to love each other deeply. This nervousness I feel around him, when my stomach goes all aflutter must be what it is to fall in love. I'll be glad when we're married and it settles. Why, I haven't had a moment of relaxation since I arrived.

She wrapped her arms around herself and rubbed her arms. What she would have given to be able to talk to Lilly this night before the wedding.

I shall write to her now and then perhaps she will not seem so far away.

Taking out pen and paper, Isabella sat down to write a letter to each of her friends from Lawrence, Massachusetts. She would begin with her closest friend and former roommate, Lilly.

My dearest Lilly,

I hope my letter finds you blissfully happy and beginning to settle in to your new life with your new husband. I am looking forward to hearing all about your wedding. I hope it is all you have dreamed of and that he is kind to you. I miss talking to you before going to sleep and sharing our stories and our hopes and dreams.

Ohio is more lovely than I'd dreamed with all its trees and I know it will be beautiful, come Spring. There are red birds here called cardinals who are the most colorful and cheerful of any birds I have seen. They are a dash of cheer on these gray wintery days as the colorful leaves are falling so rapidly and reminding me of how everything must end. But I must keep my spirits up and now I have these little birds to cheer me and welcome me to my new home.

I am so far removed from a big city that I feel I shall be most happy in my new home here in Yellow Springs. It is a small village, which was founded only sixty-five years ago in 1825. This may not seem like such a new village to most Americans but compared to

Europe it is quite different and the village itself is also quite different.

One hundred families settled here in that year following Mr. Robert Owen in a communitarian effort so it is quite different than any place I have ever visited or even heard of. There is racial tolerance and a friendliness the villagers have. Everyone is so nice to me.

There are many farms here and Antioch, which is a small college, has only been here for forty-eight years. Everything here seems new and shiny yet there are also the beautiful countryside's, the fields and the forests nearby. There will be much to discover on my walks. I do hope my new husband will enjoy taking walks with me once we are settled in and I start exploring.

Donald is so handsome I cannot imagine why he is not married already. He is tall and when I look up at him he makes me feel small and delicate. He treats me like a delicate flower he is afraid of crushing and that makes me feel beloved. There is such intensity to his dark brown eyes that I can hardly look away from him and you know how shy I can be. His hair is dark and thick and so different from my own blonde wisps. We seem to be opposites in every way. What a pair we shall make when people see us together.

He has been quite generous with me, beyond what

he sent before my journey. I'm afraid all did not go well for me after you and I parted at the station.

Two men nearly abducted me and would have succeeded, if not for the man who saved me from a fate I do not wish to imagine. Tom saved me but was unable to save my purse, which contained all of my money, so that when I arrived to meet Donald I arrived penniless. I was afraid he would not take it well for a moment but his response quickly reassured me.

As you know, I had hoped to wear mother's wedding dress and felt this even more so after the money he sent me was stolen, but he wouldn't hear of it. He insisted on buying me a new and more modern gown for he insists on the best of everything for me and he cares much about his position.

I wish you could see how elaborate this gown and all its accompaniments are. I feel like a small doll in it or perhaps a princess from another land.

One day I shall pass this dress on to my daughter if we are blessed to have one. Beautiful as this one is, I still wish I could wear mother's dress and feel the comfort of my family heritage and their love around me. But I must do all I can to be a proper wife for him and make him proud.

His manners are impeccable and he has a way of flustering me so that I cannot think for the confusion. Perhaps this is what it is to be in love. Having never been in love before I do not know, but surely this is what the poets write of.

Everything has happened so fast since we parted, Lilly, so much you cannot imagine. I hope to be settling down soon into my new home with my new husband and a peaceful, quiet life.

Everything about him is perfect.

I don't know why I am so nervous about getting married. Sometimes my stomach lurches at the thought and I can barely eat so much as a nibble. But perhaps all new brides feel this way, before the wedding, especially when they have just met their groom just a few days before the wedding.

Oh, do please write to me soon and let me know how things are with you. I miss you and our long talks into the night. While Mr. Donald Jenks is the kind of husband a young girl might dream of, I cannot speak as freely to him as I can to you. No matter how far we are, you shall always remain the sister of my heart.

Yours truly,

Isabella Britta Stolt

P.S. Soon to be Mrs. Donald Jenks. Isabella Britta Stolt Jenks does seem a bit long. Isabella Jenks has an unusual sound to my ear, but I suppose I shall get used to it.

Finishing her letters to Lilly, Tabitha, Hope, and Trinity, she sent one of the resort employees to post them. Wondering how her friends were faring, she hoped to hear from them soon and hoped they were as fortunate in their new husbands as she was.

~

RED ROSES and white ribbons filled the Yellow Springs Methodist Church. An elderly man Isabella had never met played the organ and the wedding march began.

Isabella stood looking at the church pews full of people she hadn't met before she started down the aisle.

She walked down the aisle alone. Slow step by slow step.

She wished she had her father's Bible in her hand along with the simple rose bouquet. Instead she had the fancy new Bible Donald had given her. Because everyone was watching.

I have no family or friends that can attend. Everything and everyone here is his. There's nothing of me, nothing of my family here with me.

Every person gathered here was someone Donald knew and most seemed to be business associates. Upper society types and their wives.

There were more people sitting inside the

church looking at her than Isabella had expected. Suddenly her shyness became overwhelming. Her face heated and she had to fight the urge to look down.

Instead she moved her gaze to Donald and tried not to look at anyone else. All these strangers she didn't know were watching.

Donald's eyes carried a heat and he kept an encouraging smile on his face as he looked back at her.

Oh he is so handsome. Everything is happening so fast.

Her belly gave a flutter of nerves and for one fleeting moment she almost stopped and turned away from him, the doors of the church right behind her closer than her groom who stood waiting.

She paused.

Everything and everyone here is his. There is nothing of me here. Not even the smallest thing. Everyone and everything here is his and soon I will be his too.

She started to panic.

I don't have to do this. I don't have to go through with the wedding. I could turn and run, right out those doors.

But then he smiled at her and held out his

hand and within that moment, she did have to go through with it.

I told him yes. I promised to marry him.

And so she took that next step forward. The moment of doubt was gone, as she pressed on, one step forward after another, fighting her nervousness and uncertainty.

It simply made sense to do this. Everything would work out. It was only nerves.

She barely heard the organ as it played. His smile broadened as she neared him and she smiled in return, lost in his smile.

The ceremony went by in a blur of words spoken and rings exchanged. Everything was happening fast, as if within a dream and tonight they would consummate their marriage.

Then they had each said, "I do" and been pronounced husband and wife.

Suddenly the rush was on to their house for the reception where there would be cake and champagne toasts.

At last all the guests had gone and Isabella could step out of the wedding slippers, which had begun to pinch her feet.

Dolcinda, Isabella's lady's maid, helped Isabella remove the heavy wedding gown and then carried the gown out, leaving her only in her underclothing.

Donald entered the room, his eyes bright and a glass of brandy in his hand. He stopped just inside the door, closed it and locked it. Then, pocketing the key, he approached her with a smile.

Sitting on the dressing table stool, Isabella blushed beneath his gaze and her eyes dropped to the carpet, suddenly feeling shy.

"Nervous?" His voice had a different tone tonight.

"Yes," her voice came out almost in a whisper.

He now stood before her and took a sip of his brandy before offering her one as casual as anything. As if she were not sitting in their room without a dress to cover her. "A bit of courage for you."

"Oh I don't usually drink the stronger spirits and I've already had two glasses of champagne. There were so many toasts. I'm a bit tipsy, I confess."

Donald certainly had encouraged them in their toasting. Now he sat watching her. He held the glass out toward her. "Just this once won't hurt you."

She took the glass from his hand and took a sip. The brandy was of course too strong for her, as she knew it would be, but she swallowed anyway. Anything to calm her stomach that was turning over and over again more than it had in the church.

"You barely ate today. Like a bird." His tone scolded her.

Perhaps he was concerned.

"I was too nervous to eat."

"That was quite noticeable. In the future I'll expect you to eat whether you are nervous or not. I won't have people saying my wife is wasting away. That she is unhappy."

"Yes." She paused. "Donald." It sounded so foreign on her tongue. She took another sip.

He hadn't asked for the glass back and with his scolding her nervousness had increased. It was said consummation could be painful for the woman. Perhaps she should finish the glass.

He stood watching her without speaking.

Holding the glass, her thoughts scattered, reaching for something familiar. Everything about her new home was new, as well as the way he was looking at her. She had to re-gather her thoughts. He expected her full attention this night.

Oh, why did I agree to marry a man I didn't know?

This is so much harder than I thought it would be. He is handsome and I should want this. Any woman would be lucky to be married to him and I do want to have children.

"I might need more time," she spoke, her voice low, ashamed to show her nervousness.

"More time." He sat in a chair directly across from her and leaned back, his legs wide, his glass resting on his right leg. Even seated in a chair and not towering over her, he had a commanding presence.

What would he do? Her stomach did another flip.

"I'm not the sort of husband who will wait weeks for his new bride to come around to the idea of being bedded. The first time is best dealt with quickly, that the difficult part should soon be over for the woman and then the difficult part is past and done. Delaying will only build fear in your mind, my dear. And I won't have that." His voice brooked no argument.

Wide eyed, she took another sip of the brandy, hoping it would settle her nerves.

He nodded at her glass. "Now drink up. Until you finish it."

She raised it to her lips for another swallow. The strong spirits were making her feel warm now and perhaps this was best. She needed to settle her nerves.

"When you have finished, go lie down on the bed."

It didn't occur to her that she had any choice but to obey. This was what good wives did and she'd just vowed to obey her husband as they took their vows before God.

He sat quiet in the chair watching her with intensity as he sipped from his own glass.

Once she'd emptied her glass she did exactly as he said. He didn't speak, but set his glass down and walked over to where she lay on the bed and began unbuttoning his sleeves as he watched her.

CHAPTER 8

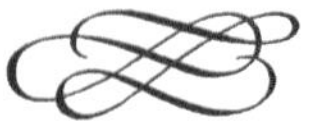

One of those little red birds sat on a branch outside the bedroom window, singing with the rising of the sun. Isabella didn't want to wake up this morning and flung an arm over her eyes.

The day is too bright. The sounds are too loud.

Pulling the covers over her head, she wished she could stay here in the warmth of the bed for as long as possible. She ached. Deep in her heart. Dried streaks of her tears still lay upon her face.

Before last night, there'd been an awareness that marital relations might be difficult. It was understood that after the first night things would improve and they could build an intimacy of love and devotion as they worked upon improving their time together.

She had expected afterward he would be kind to her and show her some sort of tenderness.

She'd reached out to him with her hand as she spoke in a low soft voice, "Please, hold me."

He turned away.

She caught her breath, tears forming.

He flung on his robe, grabbed his glass of Brandy and the decanter and headed downstairs, leaving her alone.

Curling onto her side as tears fell upon her pillow; she vowed never to beg to be held again. She pulled the covers up over herself and slept.

Oh why did I drink all that brandy last night after having champagne? I feel positively awful this morning, as if I'd been poisoned.

She didn't even want to get out of bed this morning, so she stayed beneath the covers hoping she'd fall asleep again. Even the cheerful cardinals couldn't cheer her today. Though she could hear movement and voices downstairs, no one came upstairs to disturb her.

Mid-day when she finally arose and dressed to go downstairs in search of some bread and cheese to eat, she met Mrs. Blevins coming up the stairs.

"If you were waiting for Dolcinda to help you

dress, she has been let go," she said. "You'll have to tend to yourself now. I'm no lady's maid."

"I'm used to tending to myself," Isabella answered, remembering Donald had hired her for one day. "I've no need for a lady's maid."

Mrs. Blevins turned to go down the stairs.

"Wait, please," Isabella said.

The woman stopped and turned back to look at her.

"The cake yesterday was delicious," she said. "Everything was. And you did it on such short notice. I can't imagine how you put everything together with just a few days notice."

"Not at all," Mrs. Blevins answered. "Mr. Jenks has been planning this wedding for over a month." She gave Isabella a strange look and then continued on down the stairs.

A month? But I didn't even say yes until a few days ago. He must've been very sure of himself to make plans before I did.

Donald was in the parlor reading. He closed the book when she entered. "Ah. You are up. Good." He nodded. "Before supper I'll take you for a walk." He smiled, his eyes kind. "If you are up to it, my dear."

Gone was the uncaring man from last night. In his place was the charming handsome man she'd married who was looking at her in a caring way. It was most confusing.

"Yes," she nodded. "I am up to it."

She was sad and tired but it was nothing that would get in the way of a good healthy walk. The idea of being outside in the fresh air appealed to her. It would help her clear her head.

Mrs. Blevins entered the room and addressed him. "Shall I serve the meal now, sir?"

"Yes." He rose and walked toward Isabella. "I'm sure my new wife is hungry after last night." He winked and continued past her into the dining room. "I've been waiting on you. And I have a huge appetite."

Isabella followed him into the dining room and sat, wondering how she'd ever be able to eat.

The cook served a hearty beef stew and rolls, which settled Isabella's stomach and her nerves. There was something about a good stew, which made one feel at home, and Isabella wanted to feel at home.

But watching her new husband across the table, it felt as if she didn't know him at all. It was so hard to reconcile the one side of the man she'd seen with the other.

How could this be the same man who'd turned

away when she'd reached for him, begging to be held?

She said little as she ate, her mind grappling with the events of last night. She didn't know what to say to him nor was she comfortable looking at him directly.

He didn't speak to her until Mrs. Blevins brought in a bowl of hot biscuits.

"Well, Mrs. Jenks," he asked in hearty voice that nearly made Isabella jump. "Are you enjoying your stew?"

"Yes," she answered quietly. "It's very good."

"Mrs. Blevins, we both approve," Donald said. "You must make this again for us." He nodded at her.

Mrs. Blevins smiled. "Yes sir."

"The biscuits are good and hot." He handed the bowl to Isabella. "Try one."

She took the bowl from him and quietly said, "Thank you."

When he finished his stew, Donald pushed back his bowl and said, "I know just the place for your walks. It's the most scenic in the area." He stood and held out his arm. "Come. I've been waiting to show you."

Watching Donald's expression, she hesitantly

rose, threaded her arm through his, and placed her hand on it.

He closed his other hand over hers as they walked outside. "It isn't far from the house and there are only about three miles of trails to walk, but you can see the Clifton Gorge and the river. You will love the view, my dear," Donald said as they walked down the street.

The sun was shining, and the birds were singing. Isabella began ever so slowly to relax with each step. Crossing the last street they walked through a park. The trees at the edge only broke for a small footpath, which Donald seemed to know well.

Walking beneath the canopy of trees, Isabella felt as if she stepped into a different world. This was more like the forests of her homeland. Though the sights were new, it felt like home. So caught in that feeling, she barely heard what Donald was saying.

"The gorge is just up ahead. Watch your step," he said.

Suddenly, they reached one of the overlooks and stood looking down into the gorge.

"Oh," she gasped as she looked down into the rushing waters below. "It's beautiful. And so far down."

"Yes, it is." He smiled. "Very."

She held onto his arm a little tighter, her stomach getting that fluttering feeling again and a squeamishness.

He patted her hand as if to reassure her. "This overlook has a history. Allow me to tell you the story of Darnell's Leap."

"Oh yes." She smiled up at him. "Please. I do enjoy a good story."

"As you wish." He nodded and then began. "Darnell was a member of Daniel Boone's outfit. He was captured by Indians."

"Oh no," Isabella said. "How dreadful." She shivered. She'd never seen an Indian but she'd heard stories about them and how they scalped people.

"Yes, Indians. But soon after being captured, he escaped. They discovered his escape quickly and hunted him down until they caught up with him near this narrow part of the gorge." He paused for dramatic effect.

"Yes? What happened then?"

"Legend says that he miraculously leapt across the chasm to avoid being recaptured."

She looked across the chasm and looked back at her new husband. "Truly?"

"Yes, truly. According to the legend."

"My goodness. That was quite a leap."

"Indeed."

They stood looking at the chasm in silence until he finally said, "It's time to go back."

"Yes." She nodded. "Of course." She'd quickly learned he liked things to be precise and on time. "Thank you for bringing me here and telling me the story."

Perhaps he has started to care for me a little. He's made the effort to show me this walking trail and to share a story. Two of my favorite things. Perhaps he'll join me in a walk again. It would be lovely to go for walks with my husband and enjoy the beautiful sights together.

Lightened by her thoughts, she beamed a happy smile all the way back to their home.

At the front yard he said, "I trust you'll be able to find your way there by yourself from now on and won't need someone to go with you."

Though her heart fell, she kept the smile on her face. "Yes, of course. I'm used to walking alone."

I have been walking alone for so long.

Though she had a husband now, it really felt no different. It still felt as if she were walking alone.

THE NEXT DAY she was out of bed much earlier. Fortunately, he had left her alone so she could go on to sleep. Perhaps his behavior on their wedding night was a one-time occurrence and they could both move on from it. She hoped so.

At breakfast, Donald announced he had to go into town and collect the ledgers he needed in order to work at home. "You'll have the day to yourself." He smiled at her. "You and the cook can plan the menus for the week. Surprise me."

"Oh yes, of course. I will be happy to."

A whole day to herself. *How lovely.*

They'd been spending so much time together since she'd arrived and a break from him sounded good.

THE BEEF ROAST had been dry and Donald was complaining to Mrs. Blevins, the cook.

I would never speak to a servant that way.

Perhaps she could have a softening effect on Donald now that they were married. He had agreed they'd discuss the running of the household.

I must speak to him about this when we're alone. I won't contradict him in front of the servants, but he must understand that a servant can be corrected with kindness. Perhaps if I remind him that I too worked as a servant briefly and cannot bear to have them ill treated in any way he'll be kinder to them.

He was still berating the poor cook who appeared as if she might quit any moment, when a knock came on the front door. He went to answer it as the cook fled back to the kitchen.

Isabella laid her fork down, having finished her dinner and, curious as to who had come to call, followed in his wake.

Donald opened the door, saying, "May I help you?"

Isabella shifted so that she could get a better view, and then froze.

"Thomas Allenby," Tom bowed.

Isabella caught her breath.

Tom? Here to see me?

She clasped her hands together as she stood behind Donald watching and listening.

I cannot believe he's here. Really here.

"Donald Jenks," her husband replied.

Turning, he almost pulled Isabella forward. "And this is my new wife, Isabella."

"Oh we've met," Tom grinned.

Laughing, Isabella said, “Yes, we have.”

Already her new husband was frowning and likely wondering who the man was and what he wanted. Donald briefly glanced back and forth between them.

Finally, Isabella said, “Tom is the man who saved me from those men at the train station. He saved my life.”

“And now he’s here for a reward,” Donald said. “I should’ve expected as much.”

No. Thomas was not like that. But she held her tongue and kept back the words, which wanted to rush from her lips.

As if he hadn’t heard Donald, Tom held out a bag of money. “I recovered Isabella’s purse with the money that was stolen from her.”

Instantly, Donald’s demeanor shifted. “Come in, come in. We were just about to have dessert. Please, join us.” Suddenly he was the warm, welcoming host. He stepped aside with a flourish and a bow.

Isabella marveled at how drastic the change was, and even more incredibly, how fast it happened.

Why, watching him you would’ve thought Tom was a long lost friend. How quickly Donald changed.

They moved into the parlor and Isabella called

for coffee and dessert cakes to be served. She then settled on a chair, trying to hold back her excitement. Tom was her first company to visit since they had married.

"So, you're newly married?" he asked.

"Yes, just two days ago." She beamed at him; so happy he was here visiting with her. It was as if the room lit up when he'd entered. "Here in the Methodist church. All the guests were on Donald's side."

"My friends are your friends my dear," Donald said.

"Where are you from Mrs. Jenks?" Tom asked. "Your accent is Scandinavian. Norway? Finland?"

"Oh! Yes." Her face lit with pleasure at the chance to tell him more about herself. "I am from Sweden."

"Ah!" he said with a grin. "I love it when I'm right. What part of Sweden are you from?"

"Orby, Alvsborg. Orby is part of the town Kinna in Mark Municipality, Vastra Gotaland Country."

"Is it a large town?" Tom asked as he bit into a dessert cake.

"Oh no. Orby is a parish as well as a town." Isabella laughed. "There are fewer than two thousand people in my hometown." Isabella gave him a smile. "I'm not so fond of the big cities. New York City was much too big for my liking. I missed the trees."

"What brought you to America?" He leaned back in his chair and accepted the cup of coffee Mrs. Blevins brought him, nodding at her and giving his attention back to Isabella.

"There has been terrible unemployment in Sweden and American wages are higher than they are in Europe. Father was looking for a better life for us as the lack of industrial jobs there has been bad and he saw it as only getting worse. He saw an advertisement in the Hemlandt, which is a Lutheran magazine from the United States and is read in Sweden."

"He came over to take a job working as an engineer for a company in New York and brought mother and me with him. We sold everything and had planned to start a new life here, but the journey was difficult. We traveled aboard the Stockholm-Lubeck steamship service and had to take the train to Lubeck. From there on the train to Hamburg and then boarded a ship to the British port of Liverpool where we then changed to a transatlantic liner bound for New York City."

Tom raised his eyebrows in an expression of

surprise and admiration. "That was quite a journey."

"Yes it was and it was hard on my parents. The journey by sea became difficult and mother took ill first. But father caught the illness soon after."

"By the time we arrived at Ellis Island, the authorities separated us because of the quarantine. I lost them both. They never left Ellis Island. I wasn't allowed to see them before they passed, but I have the letter father wrote from both of them and I have his Bible. Both are precious to me. I've kept them with me ever since."

Donald spoke up. "It's a shame you lost your parents. But you have a new life here now. A better one." He spoke as if that was the end of it.

She didn't want to make him think she was ungrateful.

"Yes. A new life and a new beginning. This is a lovely village. The people are so friendly here. Not like New York City or Lawrence, Massachusetts."

"How did you end up in Massachusetts?" Tom asked. "That's quite a distance from New York City."

"After burying mother and father in New York City, my funds were low and I needed to take a job. I heard about the factory job in Lawrence at the mill and used most of my remaining funds to travel there and find room and board. I had only been there a few weeks when the factory caught fire and burned down."

"I heard about that fire," Tom said. "It's fortunate you weren't killed."

"Yes, I am," she said. "Very fortunate."

"Had it not been for the fire, we wouldn't have been brought together," Donald said. "And now Isabella is here, safe with me and not having to work long hours in a factory." He reached out a hand, resting it on her knee as he stared at Tom.

"Yes. This is how Donald and I met. One of the factory supervisors connected the ladies who were single with a matchmaker not far away who helps mail order brides find husbands. I met with her and sent a letter to Donald. I had found work with a very nice family but the job was only to last for one month until their regular girl returned. I don't know what I would have done next had Donald not offered for my hand in marriage." She reached her hand out for him and her husband took it, the very picture of devoted husband and wife.

Now if he would just hold my hand when we are alone. If he would just learn to be tender and show me some affection. We've only been married two days. Perhaps with time he will. This marriage is new to him too.

Tom set his coffee cup on the table next to him. “Well, I’m glad things worked out for you and I wish you both the best. Thank you for the coffee and cakes.” He rose to go.

“But of course,” she said. “Thank you for your visit and for returning Donald’s money.”

“Yes,” Donald said. “It’s most appreciated. Come back any time.”

They walked to the door and said their good-byes and then Tom was gone.

Isabella had enjoyed his visit.

How wonderful to see Tom again. I am so glad he came.

A floating, happy feeling filled her from head to toe. And Donald seemed happy as well.

I wonder if I’ll ever see Tom again?

CHAPTER 9

Isabella entered the little bookstore, excited that the village had one. With Antioch College nearby, the store was a thriving busy spot. She opened the door and stepped inside as a bell over the door jingled.

"How may I help you?" the proprietor asked.

"Oh, I shall just browse through your poetry or perhaps your shorter stories."

"Poetry is over here." The man pointed. "Browse to your heart's content. If you like mystery stories, we have the first American edition of Sherlock Holmes. *A Study in Scarlet*. It just came out."

"Thank you." She smiled and headed over to look at the display for *A Study in Scarlet*.

Not long afterward the bell over the door jingled again.

Glancing up, Isabella automatically smiled when she saw Tom.

He is still in town.

She'd seen him three days ago when he returned the money. She'd thought he'd left and she might never see him again, so this was a pleasant surprise.

Eagerly, she walked towards him.

Catching her eye, Tom smiled back. "Hello, Mrs. Jenks."

"Hello, Tom," she replied. "Thank you again for returning the money those men stole from me."

Tom shrugged. "It was nothing. I'm still sorry I couldn't make it into town for your wedding."

"Oh I would've loved to have you there," she said and gave him a large smile for it was true. She'd wished him there and but for a few days he might've been.

"I'm sure it was a beautiful ceremony. Was there a photographer? I would love to have seen you in your dress."

"No unfortunately there wasn't. I suppose my husband simply didn't think of it. There were so many details to take care of quickly for us to be wed."

"That was the wedding over at the Yellow Springs Methodist church everyone was talking about, right? With all the out of towners?"

Confused, Tom and Isabella looked around until they found the source of the question, a white-haired, bespectacled lady on the other side of the bookshelves next to them.

"Why yes I suppose it was," Isabella replied.

Tom eyed the old woman skeptically, but she didn't seem to notice.

"I thought it might have been. I know everyone in this town, but I'd never seen them before. Or you, come to think of it." She cocked her head to one side. "Or you, my boy."

Tom smiled disarmingly and offered his hand. "Tom Allenby. Pleased to meet you."

Isabella smiled to herself as the old woman shook Thomas's hand, then turned to her. "And you are, dearie?"

"Isabella St-... Jenks," Isabella replied, catching herself.

"So wonderful to meet you," the old woman replied. "I'm Patricia Gearly. Our family has lived here since the town was founded."

"It is lovely to meet you," Isabella said.

"And where do you live dear?"

"We live in the white two story house at the end of Jackson Street."

Mrs. Gearly beamed. "That's the Matthews house. I know it well. Dottie Matthews and I grew up together."

"Is she still in town?" Isabella asked. "It really is a wonderful place."

"Yes, she lives with me, now, since her husband passed two years ago. Those yellow roses in the garden are her prize winning rose bushes."

"Oh, they are lovely. I just cut some from the garden for our dinner table last night. She must love yellow because there are touches of it all through the house."

"Yes, she does," said Mrs. Gearly, nodding. "How long are you two lovebirds renting the house?"

Isabella shook her head. "Oh we're not renting the house. Donald owns the house. He's quite proud of it."

Mrs. Gearly frowned in confusion. "But Dottie told me you were renting it."

Isabella's stomach did a flip. She didn't know what to say.

Her face colored as the realization came over her and her heart sunk, taking her smile with it.

“Perhaps I misunderstood Donald,” she spoke in a low voice as her gaze drifted down away from the town busybody, embarrassed. Now everyone would know she wasn’t aware the house had been rented. “It has been a rushed and confusing week.”

I must talk to Donald about this. I must ask him if someone is mistaken, or if he lied to me. And why.

Mrs. Gearly was suddenly compassionate. She laid a hand softly on Isabella’s arm. “Oh, I’m sure it’s nothing, honey. Someone probably said something different from what someone else said. We’re all human, you know. People make a lot of mistakes.”

Isabella, feeling less embarrassed, said, “Yes, misunderstandings can happen so easily.”

How kind of Mrs. Gearly.

Misunderstandings did happen quite often. Why between different languages and different cultures all sorts of misunderstandings could happen.

“Donald has told me very little actually and we haven’t known each other long.” Isabella smiled. “He was in such a hurry to marry me. Everything was a rush from the minute I stepped off the train. I had no idea he was so anxious to be married.”

“Well there you go!” Mrs. Gearly continued. “And besides, what reason would he have to lie?”

Isabella smiled, and then glanced over at Tom. He'd been about to say something, but stopped.

"What reason would he have...?" he said, softly, frowning.

With a final pat, Mrs. Gearly turned away and continued strolling through the bookshelves.

Isabella watched her go, and then turned back as Tom touched her on the arm.

"Isabella, what has your husband told you about work?"

"Oh he is an accountant for a distillery. But he works from home now that we're married instead of going into the office. Today is the one day of the week when he goes to Dayton."

"Hmm. Really. How's business?"

"He never discusses the finances with me. But he always has the finest things and he has excellent taste. Oh, if you had seen my wedding dress, why, that alone would've taken nearly a year of my salary at the mill."

Tom nodded and seemed to speak to himself. "Yep. I'm sold." Turning back to her, he smiled, and suddenly the room was much brighter. "That's good to hear. I hope everything sorts itself out. It was so good to see you again."

She beamed at him. "Seeing you was the best surprise I've had since leaving Lawrence."

~

SHE WATCHED Donald looking through the books in his study and waited for him to notice her in the doorway. But as usual she'd been much too quiet and he hadn't heard her approach.

She stood close by his chair and cleared her throat.

He looked up at her.

Oh it is so hard to ask him this, but I must.

"I was in town today," she began.

"You went into town?" He frowned.

"Yes, to purchase a book," she said and held the book up in her hand.

He gestured to a shelf of books. "These are not sufficient for you?"

"There are no books of poetry, other than Shakespeare. Though I ended up purchasing this story about Sherlock Holmes."

"I see." The frown had not left his face. "And?"

"And I was talking to a woman I'd just met. A Mrs. Gearly."

"Mrs. Gearly." He nodded as if he knew the woman.

"Yes, and she said." Isabella took a deep breath and then came out with it. "She said our house is a rental. That a Dottie Matthews owns the house."

His eyes narrowed and he stood, now towering over her, as Isabella took a step back. "She did, did she? And what else did Mrs. Gearly say?"

"Nothing else, that was all," Isabella said.

His features relaxed again. "You must be confused by this. Which is why I didn't tell you the full details of our arrangement."

"Arrangement?"

"Yes. I've rented the house with an option to purchase it. I wasn't sure until you arrived if you'd find the house to your liking."

Isabella's brow wrinkled.

If this was so, why didn't he tell me so in the beginning? Why as far back as the advertisement he'd claimed to own a house in the country. And now to find this isn't true...

Her stomach gave a flip again.

"You must leave the finances to me, my sweet," he said. "I don't expect you to follow complicated business deals. Suffice it to say, I acquired the house temporarily, have assessed your enjoyment of it and will be purchasing it as promptly as the deal is completed." He shrugged. "The house is ours, you may decorate it as you wish and plant whatever you want. There's no need to fret over the business end of it. You do wish to live here do you not?"

"Yes, I love the house. It is everything I dreamed of."

"You were meant to live in this house and we shall have many happy years here, together. Now." He grew stern. "If there is something you wish to know, you will come to me and ask. Not be asking questions around town. Agreed? We don't want these kinds of misunderstandings."

"Agreed." She nodded. "I don't care for misunderstandings."

Or for being lied to. Had he lied? Is he lying now? And if he would lie to me about this, what else would he lie about?

CHAPTER 10

Donald made a new arrangement with the cook who now only came half days. She would cook and serve breakfast, and the midday meal, but leave before the evening meal, leaving them prepared food, but no one to serve it.

Isabella carried the tureen of soup into the dining room where she'd already set the table and placed the rolls. Then she went to Donald's study and, stepping inside said, "Everything is ready."

He turned and said, "Eat without me. I'll have something later."

"Oh, well, all right."

He turned back around without another word to her and went back to working on his account books.

Quietly she walked back to the dining room, ladled out soup for herself and sat. Dining by herself at the large table was lonely and much too quiet. It also left her alone with her thoughts.

Donald had been spending more and more time hovering over his account books. She couldn't tell if he had more work or if he was avoiding her. He remained pleasant as long as the cook was around, but after she went home, Isabella couldn't be sure of his moods. She found herself tensing up the moment the door closed behind Mrs. Blevins, leaving her alone with her husband. Then her stomach would do that strange flipping which seemed to happen more when her husband was around.

She ate half her bowl of soup, laid her spoon down and placed her hand on her stomach.

It was no use. That strange flipping feeling was back and she'd not be able to eat more.

Strange how often my stomach does that now, when it never did before I came to live here.

She got up to clear the table.

There's no point in trying to eat when I feel this way. Nothing will settle right. It is best not to.

Clearing the table she wondered what to do with the soup. It would get cold if she left it on the table. Deciding it would be best not to let his soup get cold, she returned it to a pan on the stove and turned the heat down low. Then she turned to wash the dishes.

The cook left her very little to do and she was glad to have an activity of some kind to keep her occupied. It calmed her nervousness to have something to do and kept her thoughts off of how the evening might go, whether he'd be in a bad mood, whether he would want intimate relations.

He'd not touched her since the first night. It was so strange, and she couldn't wrap her mind around it.

Did he not enjoy it? Is he not attracted to me? Could it be he's sorry for how he treated me on our wedding night?

She hoped it was the last and that one-day he would reach for her in a kinder way, that all might be well between them. She wanted to be a good wife.

The strangest thing that she could not wrap her mind around at all was his ability to be tender and good to her when others were around, yet there was this other side of him that others didn't see, and it frightened her.

That he could be good to her sometimes gave her hope it might one day be better and she clung to that hope. She prayed every night for God to do something to change her situation and for guidance to know what to do. Last night she'd resolved to go for a walk every day as that helped to clear her head.

As she washed the dishes, she wondered if she might slip away for a walk this night. It wasn't as if he wanted her company in any way. Everything about his posture and his voice had sent the message to leave him alone.

Well, that is just what I shall do. Leave him alone and go for a walk.

She hung up the apron in the corner and reached for a coat. Shrugging it on, she stepped out the back door and lingered for a few minutes among the flowers, touching one here and then one there. This was what she needed. To be outdoors, breathing the fresh air, and not thinking of all the bad things but just breathing and being happy to be alive.

She moved through the garden and then turning the corner just past their yard, she crossed the street and moved toward the Clifton Gorge Park.

Isabella's thoughts churned as she walked. It felt better to be out of the house. The air was too heavy in there with something she could not name.

Donald said and did all the husbandly things one might expect a new groom to say and do when others were around, but the minute the doors were closed again, closing them off from the world, that air descended again. That heavy air which made her feel as if something was wrong.

She walked along the path across from Jackson Street, which led to the Clifton Gorge. Heavily forested trees and the lighter cooler air, which such groupings of trees provided met her.

She stepped among ferns and tiny forest flowers, lifting her skirts and taking care not to crush them. The moment she entered and began to breathe the air here, her spirits began to lift.

Here, away from that house and her new husband she could breathe. And think.

Why had he wanted a wife?

Past bedding her that first night, his interest waned. Part of her was glad he didn't touch her in the way he had that night and part of her wished he'd be the tender and loving husband he was when others were around.

It was as if she was married to two different people. The one others saw and the one only she saw. She didn't understand what he wanted from her.

Any time she tried to leave the house, he

wanted to know where she was going. It was as if he had to know where she was every moment of every day.

The attention he lavished on her when they were out in public was nearly embarrassing. Trying to touch her and kiss her made people stare. But he'd toss it off with a "This is my new bride. Isn't she lovely?" So anyone watching them would've thought he was the most doting of husbands.

But in her heart she couldn't help but feel he did not care for her. Not to mention any thought of love. But then what could one expect when marrying a man you'd only met in a letter?

Perhaps it had been doomed from the start.

Now she was stuck here, married to him and becoming more and more unhappy every day. She'd thought all she needed was a nice little house in a small town where she could be out beneath the trees and the stars. The perfect little house was right here and she was living in it. But it had not made her happy.

The moment he walked into a room she felt the difference in the air. It was as if he carried the heaviness in with him.

If only something could change her life. Like a

miracle. She sat on a rock and bent her head to pray.

THE FRONT DOOR SLAMMED, shaking the house. Isabella gasped. *What in the world?*

The cook had gone home. She was alone in the house.

"Isabella," Donald bellowed.

He's angry.

She hurried downstairs as fast as she could to meet him, barefoot and wearing her white nightgown, not taking the time to throw on her robe or slippers.

She reached the bottom of the stairs and hurried to the front door where he stood just inside, glowering.

He took three heavy strides toward her and she stepped backward until a wall was at her back. Donald now towered over her, anger filling his face. "My faithful wife," he growled.

Isabella's eyes widened and she froze, frightened all the way to her toes.

He grabbed her by the arm, his fingers digging deep into her skin. "You neglected to mention your meeting with Thomas," his deep whisper made her fear him even more.

"W...what?" she stammered, her heart racing. "I don't understand."

He tightened his grip. "Questioning me." He grabbed her other arm. "Questioning me as if I was not honest with you." Holding both her arms tight, he shook her as he shouted. "Did you think I wouldn't find out?"

She cringed as he shouted but couldn't pull away as he held her so tightly. "No," she protested not understanding what he was angry about.

He sneered. "You must know there is nothing you do that I won't find out about." He shook her again and her head banged against the wall behind her.

"Please stop," she said. "You're hurting me."

"You should have thought of that before you met your lover."

"My what? No, you're wrong. I don't have a lover. I haven't met anyone."

"Mrs. Gearly saw you."

Oh. The bookstore. Tom.

He saw her expression change.

She'd never been able to hide what she was feeling or thinking.

His eyes shone with the knowledge he'd hit upon a truth.

"That town busy body knows everything that goes on in this town. And now everyone in town will know about you and your lover."

He'd gripped her arms so hard she couldn't feel her fingers. "Please let me go."

"You're my wife. I'll let you go when I choose to."

"You're hurting me," she whispered.

"You spread your legs for that Allenby?" He slammed her back against the wall as if she hadn't spoken and then pressed his body against her and said, "You are mine." He leaned in and spoke into her ear. "You hear me? Mine."

She nodded. "Yes," she whispered. "Yours."

"Remember that, wife."

"Please," she whispered, closing her eyes, as a tear rolled down and then another. "Let me go."

"Look at me."

She opened her watery eyes and looked into his cold gaze.

"I will warn you but once. Stay away from Allenby and Mrs. Gearly. There will be no more trips to town by yourself as I cannot trust you to so much as visit a bookstore."

"Yes, whatever you want. I promise."

Anything to make him let her go. *Anything he wanted.*

He gave her one last shake before releasing her and stepped back. Then raking her body with his gaze he gave her a look of contempt and a sneer. "Get to bed."

She turned and ran up the stairs, holding her nightgown up with one hand and barely holding back sobs of fear and release as she clutched for the bannister all the way up with her other hand. Hurrying into their bedroom she closed the door with shaking hands and leaned back against it listening for his step.

He wasn't following. Oh thank God.

She hurried over and climbed into bed and then pulled the covers up, praying he wouldn't come to bed and take more of his anger out on her in some other worse way.

What had Mrs. Gearly said to him? Tom and I are not lovers. We've never so much as kissed.

She curled onto her side in a small ball and held the covers tight, her fingers now having feeling again. Her head ached from where it had hit the wall and her arms were sore from his rough handling of her. Her hands clutching the covers shook slightly and she tried to calm her breathing and thoughts.

Tom and I have never so much as kissed. There was that moment at the train station. That moment when I wished he had. Wished he'd kissed me.

Would I now be married to Donald if he had?

I wish Tom had kissed me then, before I got married. Just once. One kiss.

She closed her eyes remembering how it had felt those brief moments, to be in Tom's arms. How safe and warm and cared for she'd felt. Something she now knew she'd never feel within her husband's arms. Whether it was a change in behavior from his drinking or from his temper or anything else, his mood changes were something she would fear from now on.

I will never feel entirely safe with Donald. Not after his terrible temper this evening. I must make sure I do nothing to raise his jealousy again. This means I cannot see Tom again, not even by accident.

The tears she'd held back came now and she sobbed into her pillow. Her arms were sore from rough handling, her head hurt and she'd never felt so alone in her life.

This time there was no Tom to save her. He'd be long gone, now that he'd delivered the money, and even if he wasn't, she dared not speak to him without her husband there. No, no one could save her. She was married to a man so very different from the man she thought she'd married, but no one would ever believe her if she tried to explain the side of him that only she could see.

He's so charming around everyone else. He has everyone fooled. And now people in town will think I'm a bad wife, taking a lover, when that's the farthest thing from the truth. I'll be ostracized by the society people he knows. And I have no friends in this town. There's no one I can talk to about this. No one.

DONALD GAVE another swirl of brandy, and then took a big gulp, followed by a deep breath. He glanced around the room again, looking for the men with whom he'd corresponded, but had never met. A friend of a friend had put him in touch with these people, and now Donald regretted having so many degrees of separation. He was trusting too many people with too many details.

The brandy wasn't helping. His hand shook as his pocket watch tick tick tick tick ticked the seconds away. Donald had arrived ten minutes before the scheduled time, and now he'd been waiting for twenty.

With a final swig, he swallowed the last of the brandy, and then dug into his coat for his wallet.

"Looking for this?" Came a voice over his shoulder.

Startled, Donald turned to the booth behind him. Two men were sitting there, watching him. The older of them was holding Donald's wallet.

"Always watch your back, Mr. Jenks," said the man as he laid the wallet on the table.

Donald came shakily to his feet and sat down in their booth quickly. "How did you get that?"

The older man pointed a thumb to the younger man sitting next to him. "One of my boys here took it when he bumped into you before you came inside."

Donald glanced at the two men, then slowly picked up his wallet and put it back inside his coat. His sense of fiscal responsibility was screaming to count the money inside, but his sense of prudent self-preservation won out. "I'm impressed. Your reputations are well founded."

The man shrugged. "How can we help you, Mr. Jenks?"

With a deep breath, Donald put his head down, his hands on his unsteady knees under the table. "My wife."

At that, the man almost chuckled. "Why am I not surprised."

Donald nodded. "Yes, she's–"

"I don't care, Mr. Jenks," the man said, holding up a hand to stop him. "The less I know, the better, and the less you know about our work, the better. Understand?"

There was a tense pause, during which Donald swallowed, and then nodded.

Slowly, the man put his hand down and loosely clasped them again on the table in front of him.

Donald noted how relaxed the man looked. There wasn't a taut muscle in his body. He may as well have been reading a good book.

"Now when would you like this done?"

"As quickly as possible. Please."

The man arched an eyebrow. "That may make things difficult. What can you tell us about your wife?"

Beside him, the younger man took out a folded piece of paper and a pencil.

Donald eyed him suspiciously for a moment, and then said, "She likes to take walks. In the woods near the house."

"And where exactly is your house, Mr. Jenks?"

Donald looked him in the eye and finally said, "Close to Clifton Gorge."

"Ah," the man replied, leaning back. "I see you've already put some thought into this."

Donald nodded, but said nothing, so the man continued. "Now I'm assuming you want this to look like an accident."

"If she's even found at all. It's a rather remote place."

"It is," the man acknowledged. "Which will undoubtedly save us some trouble and probably save you some money. Speaking of which..."

"Yes, yes," Donald replied nervously. "Name your terms."

The man studied him for a moment before replying. "Given your requests for expedience and the staging of accidental circumstances, the price is going to be slightly more than what you perhaps had imagined, Mr. Jenks."

Donald gave a dismissive wave of his hand. "Nonsense. I've provided you with the perfect place and opportunity. All you have is to do the thing."

The man gave a small, slow nod. "Taking these into account, your price is up, but not so high as it might've been. All told, I believe your total is somewhere around the figure of... Five thousand. All of it in advance."

Donald bit his tongue and inhaled sharply, his eyes snapping at the figure.

"I had thought the deed could've been done at

closer to something like a thousand. I can give you that much right now, plus another fifteen hundred afterwards."

The man's eyes narrowed. "Don't insult us, Mr. Jenks. We're not the sort of people whom you'd like to have angered. Four thousand. Three now, one after."

"She's a seventeen year old girl, not a damned lumberjack," Donald spat. "She's nothing more than a mere slip of a thing. She could be blown off the edge by a strong wind."

"Then you do it, Mr. Jenks," the man said calmly. "You go right ahead and save yourself the money by getting those hands of yours red."

Donald stopped. For a moment, nothing in the world moved. In that instant, Donald saw himself doing it.

He felt Isabella's slight shoulders under his hands, the pressure building against his palms as he took a step forward and shoved. He felt her resist him, then fall forward. He saw her turn toward him, her big, blue eyes surprised and terrified, her arms stretching out to him, fingers grasping. Wisps of her hair had come loose, swirling in the air around her head and face. In his mind, there was a yelp of surprise, then a long, ear-splitting shriek that didn't stop until it was cut off at the bottom.

Across from him, the man stared hard into his eyes and Donald gulped.

The man, knowing what Donald was thinking, gave a few small, slow nods. “That, Mr. Jenks. That right there is why the price is what it is.”

Shuddering, Donald sighed. “Two thousand now and the rest after.”

“Done,” the man said.

CHAPTER 11

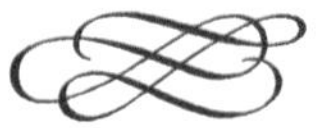

Donald had that brooding look on his face again. The one that made her hesitate to ask what was wrong.

She climbed the stairs to their bedroom, avoiding him and hoped the evening would be peaceful for a change. Outside thunder boomed off in the distance announcing a storm moving in. For a brief moment, Isabella wondered how bad it would be, and then relaxed, almost with a smile.

This isn't the East Coast anymore. No more north-easters.

Sitting at the dressing table she began to take her hair down, laying the pins on the table and starting to undo her braids.

The quiet downstairs was almost too quiet.

She'd set out his dinner as he'd requested. Hopefully he'd require nothing further from her this evening.

Her hair now down, she began to brush out her long blonde hair, enjoying the free feeling of having it out of her braids and starting to relax as she began to work through the waves now in her normally straight silky hair.

"Isabella!" Donald roared.

She jumped, dropping the hairbrush, which hit the dressing table and then the floor with a clatter. She stood and hurried to the door.

He roared her name again.

She'd never heard him this angry before. Running down the stairs her heart pounding she nearly tripped but grasped the banister on the way down, catching herself. At the bottom of the stairs she stopped, out of breath, and then gathered herself and walked into the dining room, hoping to appear calmer than she felt.

His cold, dark gaze met hers across the dinner table.

She froze.

"What is this?" He pointed to the soup tureen.

"A-artsoppa." she stammered.

Then, realizing she'd lapsed into Swedish, she corrected herself. "Yellow pea soup."

He continued staring at her, his brow darkening further.

"It's made from peas, water, salt onions, and herbs." She continued in as cheerful a manner as she could, as if by being cheerful she could change his mood.

Still, he said nothing and continued to stare.

Wavering in her cheerfulness, still she continued on. Perhaps if she explained. "I thought since you enjoyed peas with your dinner, you would enjoy the soup."

His face turning red, he rose up, knocking his bowl from the table, the soup flying everywhere. "How dare you serve me this pig slop!"

Grabbing the soup tureen, he hurled the vessel at the wall and she flinched as he flung plates, soup splattering everywhere, green spots of it hitting her cheek, her hair, and her dress.

China shattered on the wall behind her.

"I'm sorry!" she cried. "I didn't mean–"

"Sorry you are! Sorry excuse for a wife." He came around the table toward her, his voice rising with each word.

She stepped backwards, shards of plate crunching beneath her feet, making her balance unsteady.

Backing up as fast as she could, her feet scrambling across the broken china, she felt behind her for the wall, instinctively searching for the doorway, the exit, the way away from him and his anger. Fingers feeling that wall touched wet soup on the wallpaper as one hand met the splatter. She kept moving, while each step he took toward her seemed more menacing. Her breath came shorter and shorter until she felt she nearly could not breathe.

I have to get out of this house.

The moment she found the doorway with her hands she turned to run through it into the kitchen. Grabbing her coat off the hook by the back door, she ran outside without pulling it on. Wind whipped around the side of the house and she shivered at the sudden chill. A few miles off thunder boomed again as the storm moved closer. She ran, jamming one arm into the coat and racing away from the house, stopping only long enough to slip into the other arm. Then she was off, running away from the house, running until she reached the corner of their street and realized he wasn't following after her.

She slowed her run to a walk and tried to catch her breath while darting looks over her shoulder. The air was heavy with the approaching rain but she would not return to that house. Not now while he was so angry. She wiped her hand across her face where the soup had landed but it had dried. It was in her hair. She held back a sob.

As she moved across the street toward the trees, she realized no one was about to follow her. She began to calm as her breath steadied. Out of habit, she moved into the steady rhythm of walking which had always been her way to calm herself. Ever since she'd been a child, when she was upset she would go outside for a walk, so she fell naturally into the pattern of her youth and did what she always did when distressed.

As she walked, her thoughts moved away from her new husband's behaviors to the sights and sounds of her walk. Usually her distress and aggravation gave way to the rhythm of her walk and her mind would clear.

Tonight it did not.

A drop of rain fell on her forehead.

Running was what she'd done, what she was still doing, even though anyone watching her would only have seen her walking. In her heart and her mind she was running.

Moving briskly she soon reached the favorite part of her walk, the part which led to Clifton Park and the Gorge just as raindrops began to fall on her a few at a time.

Dark clouds moved in and visibility changed as rain started to fall. Still she would not turn back and go back to that house. Not to that callous, distant, and demanding man who was now her husband.

Oh what have I done? To be married to such a man. A man who screams at me and throws plates. An entire bowl full of soup. What kind of man does that? He cannot control his temper. He is a man who will lay hands on me in anger. It isn't safe to be near him when he is angry like that.

She rubbed her arms, still tender from where he'd grabbed her and shook her the last time he'd lost his temper. She had a bump on the back of her head from where he'd banged her head into the wall.

He doesn't care what I want or how I feel. He doesn't care if he hurts me. From the moment he put the ring on my finger, he started to change. But no one would ever believe me, because no one sees how he really is. And who would I tell? Even if I wanted to tell someone, who would I tell? Lilly had said I could come to her if I got into trouble, all of us talked about it, but I haven't heard from a single one of them. Perhaps they don't care either. They've moved on. They have new lives and have forgotten all about me. There's no one I can tell and nowhere I can go.

The rain poured down around her, dripping through the trees leaves and open spaces in between, drenching everything. So caught up in her thoughts she moved on, uncaring that her unbrushed hair, tumbling down around her shoulders was now wet. The rain, washing the soup away from her face and hair left her chilled and she started to shiver.

Moving through the trees along the path she followed the trail, which was now familiar to her. The path beneath her was slick with rain, but she paid little attention to it as water trickled from her head down her face and the first tears began to fall.

Marrying Donald Jenks had been the worst mistake of her life. It was done now and she had to live with the consequences.

The reality of life as Mrs. Jenks was so far from her childhood dreams as to be almost unrecognizable. The only match being the house and the beautiful garden, which likely were not even hers. His presence in the house rendered even those unrecognizable so that she couldn't even take joy in them now.

Whatever benefit of the doubt she'd given to him, he chipped away at nightly, along with whatever hopes she'd been holding out that he could change.

He wouldn't change. If anything he grew worse, not kinder. Nothing I do is right, in his eyes, from the way I dress to the way I cook. Even the way I eat.

He'd claimed just the other night that he had no desire to dine with her in the evenings because he couldn't stand the way she chewed. Slow as a cow, he'd said.

She couldn't help that she had trouble eating when he was around and swallowing her food with him watching her was now difficult. The only meals she had come to enjoy were the ones she ate alone at the dining table before he finished his work.

It was so difficult to smile and pretend everything was fine when Mrs. Blevins was there and he was watching her in silence from across the dinner table.

Tears flowing more freely, her movements now slow, she walked deeper into the woods and closer to the Gorge. There she would stop and rest.

She would find her resting spot and stay there for as long as it took to feel right again. If ever such a thing could be. The rain, which cleansed so much of the natural world, was this night doing little to clear away the things she most needed cleared away.

She paused by a tree, placing her hand on it and prayed.

Please, God, I don't know what to ask but please take all the bad things away.

For several moments she stayed silent, motionless. Then she opened her eyes and continued moving along the path.

Nothing would happen, nothing would change.

She felt God was no longer listening. She moved on, chilled from the rain and nearly numb from feelings, not seeing what she passed or paying attention to her surroundings.

When she reached the Gorge overlook, she stopped, as was her habit, hardly remembering how she had gotten there. She stood listening to the rain and the river below. The water was high and rushing from the rain they'd been having this season.

Cold and tired, she felt no comfort in her normally relaxing spot. Her despair deepened. There was no anger. There was never anger. Long ago, she'd learned that ranting and raving on her own behalf changed nothing, and only made her look and feel foolish, like a child throwing a tantrum.

Despondent, she turned away, and then froze.

A man was there.

The horrible, gut-wrenching fear that it was Donald brought her heart into her throat, but it wasn't him. This man was shorter, hairier, and didn't dress nearly as well.

Isabella relaxed, but only just. She didn't know this man, and he was walking toward her.

"May I help you?" she asked.

Chillingly, the man didn't answer, but continued to walk forward.

Isabella took a step back, knowing the Gorge was only a few yards behind her, but the man continued forward. Fear rose up again.

The man was within fifteen feet of her when, from one side, another man slammed into him, knocking him away.

The first man stumbled for a few feet while the second man looked at Isabella, asking, "Are you all right?"

Before she could reply, the first man turned back with a growl, a knife in his hand.

The second man made to reach under his own coat.

But the first man was too fast, stepping close, slashing the air.

The second man dodged for a second or two, then landed a jaw-cracking punch across the man's face. The man held onto his knife, but stumbled to his knees.

The second man went to kick him, but his leg was caught and they fell together.

Now they were wrestling, the one man trying desperately to keep the knife away from him while the other kept rolling, fighting to get on top and control.

Isabella screamed, "Stop! You'll fall!"

Hearing her, the man without the knife gave a sudden, terrific heave, and the other man was thrown off again. Too close, his hand went over the edge and his weight followed it.

And it was over. They heard a short scream before he hit the bottom.

The other man frantically scrambled away from the edge, his eyes wide, his breath coming in big gulps.

Isabella stared at him, her hands on her face.

Finally, he looked at her and stood.

She stepped back, primed to run for her life, but he held out his hands. "Isabella, it's me. It's Tom."

For a moment, she said nothing.

He sounded like Tom, but this man had a mustache and beard.

Tom was clean-shaven. He wore a bowler hat,

but it had lifted, and didn't shade his eyes as it had when he'd asked if she was all right. Then she saw one corner of the moustache had lifted away.

Was it fake?

She looked closer. Those were Tom's eyes.

Their eyes met and she knew it was he.

"Tom? Tom, what are you doing here?" She rushed to him now, trusting him instantly, desperate to feel something.

Instinctively, he held her at arm's length, wanting to embrace her, but having to explain things. "Isabella, you need to come with me right now."

"What? Where are we going? We should go to the police. That poor man–"

"Was sent to kill you."

Isabella gasped.

CHAPTER 12

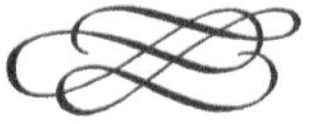

"But why?" Confusion and fear filled Isabella's wide blue eyes.

Tom was stripping off the rest of his disguise and tossing it on the mantelpiece.

Isabella watched him as he stood in front of the fire.

The first things to go had been the ridiculous bowler hat and the torn dirty overcoat. After that, he'd removed his tie and opened his shirt before pulling off the fake beard and mustache.

She watched him, somewhat relieved to see the real Tom emerging from beneath the disguise. This was the Tom she knew.

They'd run or walked through the woods until coming to a street in the darkness. Many times they'd stopped, Tom making sudden turns to look behind them or listen for any sounds, but the rain made that difficult.

Isabella, not understanding why anyone would try to kill her, had put her trust in Tom and run, following his instructions, though she wanted answers. She trusted him with her life.

But now, here, it was safe and the questions wouldn't wait.

Tom had brought her to a room on the second floor of a hotel. They'd used a staircase behind the building to get to the room, which Tom unlocked, then locked again, once they were inside.

"Why would anyone try to kill me?" Isabella asked.

Tom sighed, then went over to a cabinet in a corner and pulled out a bottle with two glasses. Pouring the drinks, he put the bottle back, then turned and offered one of the glasses to her. "Here. Sit down."

She accepted the drink and sat.

Tom sat also, across from her, in a wooden chair next to the fire. Taking a drink, he breathed deeply.

"Isabella, it's..." Tom sighed. "Maybe I should start where I began researching."

"Wait," Isabella said. "There's something else I have to know first."

Surprised, Tom asked, "What is it?"

Isabella took a breath, and then looked him in the eye. "Who are you? What do you do for a living? You said you were something like a constable. What does that mean?"

Tom looked at her for a moment, then took another drink and put his glass down on the floor beside him. Running his fingers through his hair, he said, "Okay. I'm not really supposed to talk about this, but you've been through a lot and deserve to know."

Isabella sipped at her drink, waiting for him.

Finally, Tom said, "I work for a company called Pinkerton's. We're licensed as private investigators, but lately, many police forces and even Washington have been using us to gather information."

"We research, we infiltrate, we report, and if there's imminent danger, we intervene. Sometimes it's a matter of double-crossing another organization so that they can be stopped. Other times, like tonight, we have to be quick."

Her eyes brightened as thoughts came to her making connections. "So when we met at the train station you were there on a case. And that's why you couldn't tell me."

Tom nodded. "Yes. That's exactly right. The police kept getting reports of women vanishing. We were the ones who realized they all used the same train lines, so I and many others were put in place to watch and react if we saw something suspicious."

"I'm so glad you were there that day. Oh!" Her eyebrows rose as she made another connection. "And that's how you got the money back and then you came here to return it."

Tom grinned at her, pleased that she followed so quickly. "Very good."

"But I still don't understand," Isabella said. "What does this have to do with someone wanting to kill me? How did you find out about it?"

"Okay," Tom said. "Remember the last time we saw each other?"

"Yes," she nodded.

"That day in the bookstore, Mrs. Gearly said Donald was renting the house and you said he'd told you he owned it, right?"

Again, Isabella nodded, so Tom continued. "Usually, that's not enough for me to get suspicious. As Mrs. Gearly said, people make mistakes, but I was thinking about the kind of man he was, and he didn't seem like the kind to make a mistake like that, even if it was just telling you the wrong thing. The only other possibility was that he'd lied to you."

"He is...changeable." She spoke the word slowly, giving only that little bit away.

Tom closed his eyes and swallowed.

Then he looked at her again. "That afternoon, I went to the county office to look at the housing documents. Later that night, I broke into his offices and looked at what financial records I could find."

Her hand closed around her glass as if to brace herself.

"The first thing I found was that Mrs. Gearly was right. The house is rented. That night, I found out Donald is in a lot of trouble. I think he made a mistake and saved his job by saying he could pay back the money he lost. That was when I got a really bad feeling about him and started following him around town."

Isabella rolled her eyes. "He always has to have the best of everything. The amount he spent on our wedding was far beyond anything I've seen. If he was having financial trouble why do that? And marrying me? I came with no dowry, just myself."

Tom leaned back in his chair and wiped his face with his hands. "Well, that's not all I know. Isabella, Donald's money comes from a very strange, very rare type of inheritance. His grandfather died a little over a month ago."

Right away, those words stuck in Isabella's mind, but she didn't know why. Where had she heard that before?

Words spoken echoed in her head. "Mr. Jenks has been planning this wedding for over a month."

More connections stretched toward each other in her mind as she followed Tom's words intently. "Over a month ago," she spoke the words aloud and then frowned taking a sip of her drink and swallowing hard as if that would help her accept and swallow this news down better.

Leaning forward, Tom spoke slowly. "His grandfather's will specified that his grandson, Donald Jenks, would only inherit upon his marriage. He had to accomplish that within six months while the money was held in trust. It's quite a sizable amount of money. One hundred eighty thousand dollars."

Isabella gasped.

All the connections now made, the totality of it all horrified her and she was speechless. She sat taking the brunt truth of everything in and then she rose and began to pace. "He married me so he could inherit. He never cared for me at all. Not even a little bit." Tears filled her eyes. "It was all an act. And foolishly I fell for it."

Her eyes widened and she stopped pacing to stand right in front of Tom. "But to have me killed?" She held her arms out palms open toward him and said, "I don't understand. He could've just married and kept the money. I would've made him a good wife." She gave a near sob. "I tried so hard. I would have been a good wife."

Tom nodded. "Yes. You would have. But he's not a good man."

"No, he is not." She shook her head and her voice dropped. "He's not a good man."

Remembering everything her new husband had done to her, she closed her eyes, squinting them tight.

When she opened them again she looked into Tom's eyes and let him see into hers, where dwelt all the memories of the bad things she'd been through.

Staring at her, Tom finished. "I was there when Donald hired men to kill you. That was when I abandoned him and followed them, to be certain they would try the idea they'd talked about, of pushing you into the Gorge to make it look like an accident. Then I followed the hit man and watched him as he watched your house. When you left, he followed you and I followed him, and...Well, you know the rest."

For a long moment her eyes searched Tom's. He sat silent, still, and strong. Waiting as her gaze searched his and then he spoke. "You can't go home again."

"I have nowhere to go," she whispered.

Rising, Tom held out his arms to her. It was an invitation, not a request.

Her eyes welling with tears, she stepped into his arms and closed her eyes as she leaned into him and felt them close around her, strong, warm and safe.

Tom is a good man.

He didn't make her stomach jumpy when he was around. Instead she felt calm when he was near. Safe. Like everything was right in the world. Like this was home.

"I should never have married him. I almost didn't. For one moment in the church, I...I almost turned and walked out the door. But all the people were watching and I'd promised him and so instead I walked toward him. But for that one moment..."

"Something told you to run," he said.

Isabella felt the words vibrate in his chest, soft and soothing.

"Yes," she breathed the word out, relaxing as he held her. "But I didn't know what was making me feel that. I thought it was just wedding nerves."

"Next time you should listen to that instinct. It could save your life."

"Yes," she gave a small nod against his chest. "I understand that now. So often when I was around him my nerves were on edge. Next time I will."

"Good."

Hesitantly, she said, "When I'm with you I relax and feel safe."

His arms tightened around her. "Good," he said again.

She gave a sigh as she relaxed completely, closing her eyes and breathing in, her breath changing to match his.

They stood like that for a while, her breathing in and him simply holding her and allowing her to feel safe within his arms. The terrors of the night were banished by his strength and she drew from that strength now. No, she wouldn't go home again. She'd stay here with Tom and he'd keep her safe. He'd know what to do about her husband.

She looked up into his eyes and that spark which had existed between them even when she had pushed it away, lit with a fullness that nearly swept her away.

This was the man she loved.

From the moment they'd met he'd never been far from her thoughts, just hovering on the edge of whatever called loudest for her attention.

It remained unspoken between them, but they both knew and without a word he leaned in and kissed her. Soft at first, then as that spark flared, her hands flew up around his neck as his fingers threaded through her hair, holding each other, pulling each other closer as if neither could get enough of the other.

When they emerged from the kiss, out of breath and lovingly gazing at each other, there was no doubt this was meant to be.

"I wish you had kissed me like this at the train station," she said. "I'd never have gotten back on that train."

"I wish I had too," he said. "I wanted to."

She laughed. "Why didn't you?"

He tucked a stray strand of wet hair behind her ear and, giving her a soft look, quietly said, "You were spoken for."

Coming back to reality, she took a sharp breath. "Yes, I was."

"Technically, you still are," Tom replied. Isabella noted he made no move to step back or release her.

Her forehead wrinkled as it all came crashing back at her. "Yes, I am. To a man who is trying to kill me. And I took vows." The wrinkle deepened. "Before God. I'm supposed to obey." She looked at him suddenly, wildly. "But I can't. I can't do what I vowed to do. What I'm supposed to do. I can't. If I go back..."

"You can't go back," he said firmly.

"I don't want to go back." She shook her head. "Ever." The wrinkles cleared and her eyes brightened as she spoke the words of her heart. "I want to stay with you."

Tom smiled. "I'd say you have pretty solid grounds for a divorce."

Her eyes widened. "I don't know anyone who has ever been divorced. I don't know how it is done."

Tom put a hand on her face, cradling her cheek. "Don't worry. We'll think about that later."

Relief filled her entire body. So very much had happened and she was overwhelmed by it all, but Tom would know what to do. His very presence calmed her and his touch was the kindest she'd ever known. "Yes, we can think about it later," she agreed. "There's just been so much tonight, so much since I married him..."

He touched a dried spot on her face. "What is this? On your face and in your hair?"

"Pea soup." She was covered in pea soup. She started to giggle at the ridiculous thought and the stress gave way to giggles. When she caught her breath, she spoke seriously. "He threw a whole tureen at me. He was very angry because I'd fixed him pea soup for dinner."

"So...he threw it at you?" Tom raised an eyebrow. Then he sniffed. "I shouldn't be surprised, given conspiracy for murder."

"Yes, he threw it at me. I'm just glad he didn't grab me this time. I was so afraid he would that I ran. I had to get out of that house."

TOM CLOSED his eyes and pressed his lips, trying to control the quick flash of anger he felt toward the man who wasn't here.

Giving a tight sigh, he opened his eyes again and smiled. He couldn't help himself. Isabella was that beautiful. Shining blue eyes stared up at him in perfect trust. Her cheeks, warm and soft under his hands, ached to be stroked and touched. Full red lips asked sweetly to be kissed.

Tom wanted to protect her. She deserved to be

treasured and provided for. “God’s love, Isabella,” he breathed. “If you weren’t married already I’d ask for you myself.”

“Oh Tom,” her eyes welled with happy tears, “I wish it were so and you could.” She closed her eyes and the teardrops slipped down her cheeks.

Hurriedly, his hands went to her face, wiping the tears away with his thumbs. “Don’t cry, sweetheart. I promise you, just give me a few days and this will all be over.”

Her lips parted as she breathed in beneath his gentle touch. Tom was pulled helplessly down in her eyes and he kissed her again. Longer, this kiss held a quiet, powerful strength of unspoken promises and desire. Tom held her face against his, not wanting to stop breathing her in.

When they finally parted, he swallowed, his eyes closed.

Control. She’s married. You have a job to do. Always do the job.

Opening his eyes, he smiled brightly at her. “I imagine you’d like to wash away that soup,” he said.

Her hand reached up to touch her hair. “Oh, yes, the soup.” She spoke as if she had forgotten the soup was everywhere, dried and sticky. “Yes,” she smiled. “I would.”

He nodded behind her. "There's a bathroom for you."

"Thank you," she said. Then she glanced down at her dress, splattered with soup and wet from the bottom hem up several inches. "I don't have anything to change into."

Tom's face fell for a moment. "Oh! Um... Well, I have a robe you can borrow, and..." He blushed. "It's late. You take the bed. I can sleep here." He nodded toward the chair by the fire.

"Thank you, Tom," she blushed.

Isabella's face heated at the thought of being naked beneath his robe and the fact they'd be sleeping in the same room. Oddly though, shy as she was, the thought didn't make her nervous, as it would have with any other man. She was safe with Tom. More so than she was with her own husband.

Nodding, Tom reluctantly released her.

Giving him a last blushing look, Isabella turned away as he sat down, still staring at her.

She moved toward the bathroom and paused to look over her shoulder, seeing him still watching her with an intense look in his eyes. At the doorway she stood, blushing, with her hand on the doorknob. “You mentioned a robe?”

He rose and collected the robe and then handed it to her.

As she took it from him, she thought of how he likely wore the robe with nothing on beneath it and soon she’d be doing the same. The thought made her blush deeper. “Thank you,” she whispered.

Isabella stepped inside the bathroom and closed the door, then hung the robe on a hook, and started the water running in the bath. She moved over to stand in front of the mirror and looked into it. Her hair was a wavy, wet, tangled mess with soup making it sticky. Dried splotches covered her face and neck.

How could he ever think me remotely pretty looking like this?

But she’d seen it in his eyes. Even like this, he did.

Moving away from the mirror, she removed her boots and then her dress. Eyeing it, she thought it might be salvaged if she soaked it to remove the soup stains. Fortunately, the dress wasn’t white or cream colored, but a soft shade of blue. She laid it across the chair and then removed her underthings.

Stepping into the warm bath, she felt the heat keenly against her cold toes. Easing her body down into the tub she leaned back, closing her eyes.

It is safe here to completely relax.

Something she never fully did at home in the evenings. How it felt to completely relax now suddenly made her realize how she hadn't fully relaxed like this since she set foot off the train. Since meeting Mr. Jenks.

How she hated the name now. Mrs. Donald Jenks. She couldn't wait to be rid of it. But she mustn't think of that now, or of him. She mustn't think of all the bad things.

She didn't want to think at all. Closing her eyes she simply rested and breathed.

TOM WAS FULLY aware that he'd probably not be sleeping that night. The thought of Isabella alone was enough to keep him awake. The fact that she was actually here meant he would never calm down enough to relax for sleep. That thought in mind, Tom went to his overcoat and put his hand in one of the pockets, pulling out his Colt Peacemaker.

Everything seemed to have stayed dry despite the rain. Tom laid the pistol on one of the chairs and, restless now, drew his Bowie knife from the sheath on his belt just behind his hip. There was a whetstone on the mantelpiece, which he now took down and ran over the blade, thinking about his earlier encounter as he sat in front of the fire, his elbows on his knees.

Tom had almost died again. It had happened many times in the course of his career and he was getting tired of it, even though he was only twenty-five.

At first, the rush had been addicting, combined with the knowledge that he was very good at doing bad things to bad people for a good cause.

Up until now, Tom had never questioned what he wanted to do with his life. He felt made for this.

And then Isabella had come along. Ever since the train, when he'd seen her, had pleasant conversation with her, and then rescued her, Tom had felt drawn to her. Now that he knew she felt the same way, it was enough to make him think about giving up life as a Pinkerton.

Tom had no illusions. This lifestyle was no place for a happy, carefree young marriage. If he were ever going to marry, he'd have to give up his calling.

If it were anyone except Isabella, he would never have even considered it. But for her, he would.

The thought shocked him, his hands stopped, the whetstone ceasing its harsh, sharpening scrape.

Is this...Am I...in love?

He stood up, put the whetstone back, sheathed his knife, and sat down again. After a moment of looking into the fire and thinking of Isabella's face, laughter, kiss, and sweet heart, he shrugged.

Yep. I'm sold.

FINALLY, Isabella emerged from the bathroom, wearing his robe, which she'd wrapped tightly around her small frame. Sleeves rolled, she was toweling her long blonde hair. She smiled brightly. "All clean."

He couldn't help but smile back at her.

She moved near the fire and sat, so it could dry her hair. "I feel so much better now, thank you," she said. "I was a bit chilled from the rain."

"From more than the rain, I imagine," he said.

"Yes." She nodded. "I had to rinse my dress and

it's hanging up in there. I hope it isn't in the way. It may not be dry by morning."

"Not in the way, but it would dry faster by the fire." He looked about but there were only two chairs in the room. "I'll move it in here when you go to bed. Was there somewhere you had to be in the morning?"

"Oh, I could move it." She stood to go get it.

"Sit down. It's no problem."

She sat back down. "There's nowhere I need to be. No one will expect to see me except Donald and he'll think I'm..." she didn't want to say it.

"With any luck, yes," Tom replied. "My hope is that the men he hired won't be knocking on his door asking where their man is. That means I have to work against them first." He looked at her. "Donald's going to have a good few days of not knowing you're still alive."

"Oh," her eyes widened at his explanation.

Nefarious men were so far beyond her understanding that her mind didn't think of the things they might do or how they might think.

How smart Tom must have to be to outwit men such as them.

Beyond her attraction to him and the way her heart felt toward him, was a respect that went very deep and had since the first time he'd saved her.

He was no ordinary man in her eyes. She hoped to be worthy of him.

"So you'll want me to stay out of sight then?" She tried to think of what he might want her to do.

Tom smiled at how quick she was to catch onto things. "It would be best you stay out of sight for now. I can bring food in."

"Just please do not bring in pea soup," she said. "I think I have had my fill of that."

Tom threw back his head and laughed aloud. "I imagine you have!"

She gave him a little smile and giggled. It felt good to laugh with him after the events of the evening. To be alive and to laugh and most of all, to be with Tom.

Why, he could hide her away here as long as he wanted and she would enjoy every minute of it.

When he'd stopped laughing, he looked at the clock. "We'd better get some sleep."

"Oh yes, of course." She stood. "Well, good night."

He stood and smiled at her. "Good night, Isabella. Sleep well."

She moved over to the bed and slipped beneath the covers as he sat by the fire, his pistol close by. Trying to sleep, she tossed and turned. Though she'd thought she could sleep, it soon became apparent that she couldn't. When she closed her eyes and tried to drift off, images and words came to her and she didn't know how to banish them. All the hateful things Donald had said and the ways he'd hurt her haunted. The worst of all being the men he'd hired to kill her.

It was nearly impossible to sleep knowing he and those men were still about somewhere.

"Trouble sleeping?" Came Tom's voice from by the fireplace.

"Yes. I can't sleep knowing those men are still out there and Donald wants me dead," she replied softly.

"Don't worry, honey," he replied. "For all he knows, you're nothing to worry about anymore."

"But what if those men come after me again?"

"They don't know where you are. And besides, that's why you keep me around."

"I know I'm safe with you here," she sighed, "but still, I'm having trouble sleeping. I keep remembering the bad things." She heard him stand, and then saw him as he moved closer, bringing his chair with him.

He set it near her head, and then sat down, holding out his hand.

Smiling up at him in gratitude she reached her hand out to his, and as his hand clasped hers, strong and warm, she felt secure again. "Thank you," she whispered, tears filling her eyes.

He brought her hand up and kissed it, saying, "You're welcome."

His lips upon her hand made her close her eyes briefly as happy tears began to come.

Once, before she'd reached out her hand in her need, asking to be held and had been turned away.

Tom is not like him. So different.

This time she hadn't reached out, but Tom, knowing, had reached for her hand.

Tears continued to come and she blinked them away smiling at him, unable to share what she was thinking and feeling, but hoping he might nonetheless understand what this meant to her.

Tom sighed. He couldn't stand to see her cry. "Isabella...I know you're married to someone else, but...if I promised to stay clothed and on top of the sheets...may I hold you?"

This was beyond what she could've hoped or dreamed of in this moment and her heart filled to overflowing that he would do this. That he cared that much.

"Yes, please." Was all she could get out between her tears and her heart being so full.

Slipping off his boots, Tom laid his knife and

pistol on the nightstand by the bed and went around so that he could lie down next to her. "Make yourself comfortable, sweetheart."

She shifted slightly. Feeling his arms come around her, pulling her close, she gave a soft sigh of contentment.

Everything would be all right now. She would sleep, while Tom kept away any bad men or bad dreams. Safe in his arms she slept.

CHAPTER 13

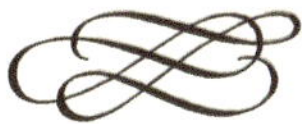

Two days after he'd thrown that horrible soup at Isabella, Donald leaned back luxuriating in his cigar, a full glass of brandy in his other hand. He had his feet up, relaxed, reveling in the thought that no news was good news.

Of course, he'd contacted the police and they'd scoured the neighborhood looking for her. The thought had crossed his mind to lead them straight to the Gorge, but that might seem a little too convenient.

The only worry he had was that the men he'd hired hadn't shown up to collect the other half of their pay.

Donald looked at the package on his desk holding the money.

Had the police caught them somehow? But no, if they had, they would have given me up as the man who hired them. Had they not done the thing yet? No, Isabella has been gone two days.

It was a mystery, but Donald shrugged, leaving it to wiser minds. The only thing he wanted to think about was his inheritance.

One hundred eighty thousand dollars. Oh, the things I could do with such a fortune! A nice large chunk of land, my own home, custom designed, of course, and all the finest things, from clothes, to cigars, to alcohol, to horses, and women. Oh yes, the women.

Donald's mind danced at the thought.

So many women, just begging to be used and paid to be on their way. I'll be able to see Katherine again. Kat likes it rough.

Remembering the last time he'd seen her, he smiled, thinking of what he'd do to her next.

Then there was a knock on his door. He almost didn't hear it, immersed as he was in thoughts of what he would do to Kat. "Who is it?"

"Mr. Jenks," came an authoritative reply, "this is the police."

Donald thumped his boots down and set his cigar and brandy aside. "One moment."

Ah, they must have found her body.

He ran a hand through his hair and loosened

his tie askew to appear haggard and unkempt. "Coming."

With a deep breath, he opened the door.

Predictably, there stood the policemen and Donald's knees buckled in mock horror. He put a hand to his face. "Have you found my wife?"

The constable, his hat in hand, asked, "May we come in, sir?"

Donald stepped aside, allowing them to enter and then closed the door behind them.

The constable continued, "Perhaps you should sit down."

"Yes. Yes of course. May I offer you men a drink? No, you're on duty, how silly of me." Donald sat, congratulating himself on appearing so disheveled.

The constable sat across from him. "I'll get right down to it, Mr. Jenks. To answer your question, yes. We've found her."

Donald sat up, playing the desperate husband to the hilt. "Oh God! Is she alive? Where is she now?"

The constable stared into Donald's eyes. "Yes. She is alive."

Donald sat stunned for an instant, his eyes wide before remembering to collapse in mock happiness. “Oh, thank goodness! I’m so sorry, I didn’t dare hope...”

“No, Mr. Jenks,” the constable continued. “I imagine you didn’t.”

Donald stood, shambling toward the brandy he’d set down earlier. Bracing himself on the desk, he tilted the glass back, downing what was left inside. “Where is she now?”

Strangely, the constable turned to one of his officers, who went back to the front door and opened it.

In horror, Donald watched Isabella walk past him, followed by Thomas Allenby, who was dragging someone along with him. There was a hood covering his face, and his hands were somehow secured behind his back.

Panicking, Donald said, “Isabella! I’m so glad you’re safe! Where have you bee–”

“Shut up, Jenks,” Thomas said. “He gave you up.”

Before Donald could ask what he meant, Thomas snatched the hood off the man he was holding. There stood the older man whom Donald had given two thousand dollars.

He took one look at Donald and said, “That’s him. He hired me and my boys to kill his wife.”

“For how much?” The constable asked.

"Four thousand dollars. He gave us half up front and was supposed to give us the other half after she was dead."

Donald balled his fists, his teeth gritted tight. "That's absurd! Who are you? How dare you make such accusations against me!"

"Sir," said one of the policemen. He came back into the parlor from Donald's study, holding the package of money. "I think this is the other half."

Donald was desperate now and everyone could see it. His eyes whipped from the money to Thomas, to Isabella, to the constable. "He's lying! I never hired anyone–"

Smack!

Donald staggered back from Isabella, who had stepped up to him and slapped him hard, open palm, across the face.

"Stop lying!" Isabella's face was furious. "At least face the consequences like a man!"

Suddenly Donald roared and lunged forward, catching Isabella by the shoulders and turning her around.

She screamed and tried to pull away.

Holding her in front of him, Donald grabbed a letter opener and held the point hard against the skin on her throat.

She went still and silent, her eyes wide as she

looked at Tom, her breath coming in short panicked gasps.

Tom let go of the man he held and the police constables made to rush Donald.

Donald yelled, "Stop!" Edging toward the back door, he said, "Don't follow me! Don't take another step forward!" With that he turned and ran through the kitchen out the back door, dragging a panicked Isabella with him.

Tom was the first after him, the policemen trying to keep up. As he ran, Tom drew his knife.

Hearing the men behind him, Donald turned and grabbed Isabella close to him again, the letter opener digging into her neck. "I'll kill her! Stop now or I'll–"

With a heave and a sharp whistle, Tom's knife flew forward, landing smack into Donald's face.

Isabella screamed and jerked away as Donald fell.

Tom opened his arms and Isabella ran to him, sobbing, her breath now coming in huge gasps. His arms closed around her and held her tight.

The policemen, gasping for breath, finally caught up with them.

The constable looked at Tom, then Donald, then back at Tom, his eyes wide. "I saw the whole thing. I've never seen anything like it."

At first, Tom said nothing, just holding Isabella who clung to him as if her life depended on it. Finally, he looked up and asked, "Am I going to be charged?"

The constable shook his head as one of his men left to get extra help. "I'll take care of everything, son."

Tom took Isabella back to the house after Donald was taken away and once they were inside and had the house to themselves, Isabella calmed enough to sit.

For a long while they did nothing but sit.

Finally, at the crack of a log and a shower of sparks, Isabella spoke. "I don't want to talk about Donald any more tonight," she said as she sat on the sofa watching the flames.

"Then we won't," Tom replied. Rising, he went over to the fire and added another log, then taking the poker, moved the logs as she watched.

"That was three," she whispered. "I should've known there would be three."

"Hmm?" He turned and looked at her. She'd spoken so softly he hadn't fully heard her.

"Three. Grandmother always said it came in threes. You saved my life at the train station, and at the gorge and now tonight. That makes three."

"What comes in threes, sweetheart?"

"Trouble. Grandmother would always start counting if there was a death in the family. She wouldn't relax until she knew what was the three, the third bad thing. Then there'd be no more trouble. Tonight was three."

"I see," he said. He came to sit beside her and put his arm around her. "Three or no three, there's not going to be any more trouble. I'll see to that."

She laid her head upon his shoulder. "I am glad there won't be. So many things have happened since I came to America. But if not for those things you wouldn't be here with me."

"That's right." He kissed her forehead and smoothed her hair. "I'm glad that I am."

"I'm glad too." She looked up at him. "Stay here with me? I don't want to stay in this house by myself."

"Yes," he said. "I understand."

"Will you hold me again tonight?"

"Of course." He hugged her close. "Any time you want. I like holding you."

She smiled. "I like it too. This is my favorite place to be. Here in your arms."

Now that Donald was dead and Isabella had the house to herself, she asked Tom to help her sort through the accounts and legal documents so she could discover exactly what her situation now was.

If Donald's financial affairs were desperate enough, she might be in a worse situation than when she'd arrived in Yellow Springs with only herself and her belongings.

But then, one day, Tom came barreling through her front door, not even bothering to knock. "Isabella!" He cried out in a happy shout. "Isabella, it's legal! It's all legal! You're not going to believe this!"

"What?" Isabella asked, hurrying out of the study.

Tom was standing in the parlor with his back to her, holding a stack of papers in his hand. As he turned, she saw the beaming smile on his face and started smiling herself, though she didn't know why.

"The inheritance! Donald's inheritance of one hundred eighty thousand dollars! He was legally married, so he got the money from his grandfather's estate, but he's dead now, so-"

Isabella's mouth dropped open and her eyes bugged, her hands flying to her face. "Oh gud!" She screamed.

Tom leaped towards her, throwing his arms around her waist and spinning her as she clung to his neck and he laughed. “If I didn’t want to marry you already I sure do now!”

“Marry me, Tom! She shrieked, stupidly happy at her amazing fortune.

Tom stopped spinning around and set her down, crushing her close in a passionate kiss. When they broke, Tom went down on one knee so hard it thumped the floor, but he didn’t even wince.

“Isabella, will you marry me?”

“Yes!” She shouted again, laughing. “Yes, Tom!”

INCREDIBLY, there was even more happiness for Isabella to find later. When going through Donald’s desk, they came across a stack of letters and telegrams addressed to Isabella.

“Oh Tom!” She looked at him, her eyes bright. “They’ve written to me! Every single one of them. They didn’t forget me.”

“Of course they didn’t.” He smiled. “How could anyone?”

She tore the letters open one right after the

other and read each through while he waited patiently.

When she finished, eyes bright with happy tears, she nearly exploded with all the news she had to share. "Tabitha went to Missouri to be with her cousin. Trinity went to West Virginia and married widower John Witherspoon. Hope went to Newark, New Jersey and married Roscoe Edwards who has an eight year old ward," Isabella said. She paused and placed her hand on Tom's arm, her blue eyes wide. "Oh but Lilly."

"The one who was like a sister to you?"

"Yes, that's Lilly. She had a narrow escape too. Lilly went to Chicago, Illinois to meet Wilber Hardesty but he didn't really want a bride. He wanted a saloon singer and upstairs girl! She escaped with the help of Seth Reagan. They married in Chicago and traveled back to Seth's Straight Arrow Ranch in Clear Creek, Kansas."

Her hand tightened on his arm. "Thomas. It's not so safe becoming a mail order bride. There are so many dangers."

"I'm glad your friends are all right. And I'm glad I got to you in time."

"I'm glad too." She smiled at him.

"You'll want to write to them to let them know what happened and that you are safe now."

"Yes. I must do that right away."

~

TAKING HER HAND, Tom asked, "Do you still love this house? Or does it have too many bad memories for you to want to live here?"

"You banish the bad things when you are near," Isabella smiled.

Tom knew this to be true, for he'd been there for enough of her nightmares, which had become less lately. "We might purchase it, if you'd like that," he said.

"Yes, Tom, I would love that," Isabella said. "Though there are things I'd want to change."

"And repair," he said, thinking of the dent in the wall and the damaged wallpaper where the soup stains had never come out. He would remove anything like that which could serve as a reminder. Donald's desk and chair had to go. His personal belongings had already been donated. Only his furniture remained.

"Perhaps we might redecorate some of the rooms," she said. "And put a gazebo in the garden." Her face lit at the thought.

Tom, who was glad to see more and more of that smile, said "Anything your heart desires."

She smiled the deepest smile of all. "That is easy, for the only thing my heart desires is you."

It took some time to sort through all the legalities.

At last everything was straightened out so that the house was purchased and Isabella and Tom could be married.

Their wedding was a small affair, with several of his family members in attendance and four of the men he'd worked with at the Pinkerton agency.

Tom assured her that she was the most beautiful bride he'd ever seen and perhaps it was the glow, for she wore her mother's dress though it was out of fashion and she carried her father's Bible, though it was worn.

Tom had insisted on it, knowing how much it meant to her to be surrounded by these pieces of her family.

Filled with the love she received from him she'd blossomed and the happiness, which shined from her eyes, made her all aglow.

Though she was more than a bit nervous on their wedding night, after Tom declared he would kiss every inch of her and banish even the ghost of a memory of what had gone before, she relaxed into his arms, knowing she was safe and very well loved.

It was no surprise to any at the wedding who'd seen the happy couple together when Isabella gave birth nine months later to their first son.

THE END

Thank you for taking the time to read Isabella, Bride of Ohio. If you enjoyed our story, please consider telling your friends and or posting a review. Word of mouth is an author's best friend and much appreciated.

Thank you!

- Debra Parmley and Robert Arrow

ABOUT DEBRA:

Author Debra Parmley likes action in her romance stories, whether she is writing a contemporary military romantic suspense, a gritty western historical romance, a sweet holiday romance, or about independent flappers in the 1920's.

Her first novel, published in 2009, in print, was a gritty western historical romance. She started out writing gunfights and still enjoys shooting long guns. The novel, A Desperate Journey, was published by Samhain Publishing in a traditional deal made through her agent after the book was selected in 2007 as one of ten novels to compete in the American Title II contest put on by Dorchester Publishing and Romantic Times Book Lovers magazine.

She went on to write contemporary romance, historical romance, futuristic romance, fairy tale romance and holiday romance for five small presses before opening her own boutique press, Belo Dia Publishing Inc. Belo Dia is Portuguese for beautiful day.

An Air Force veteran's wife, writing military romantic suspense is one of her favorites. She is a contributor to Elle James Brotherhood Protectors world and to Susan Stokers Special Forces Operation Alpha world.

An adventurous world traveler, who also sold travel, Debra often brought home folk tales and music from many countries she visited and has set foot in over thirteen countries. She escorted a group through Scotland, stayed in over the water huts in Tahiti and Moorea, and walked the plank of a pirate ship off the coast of Grand Cayman.

Debra and her husband lived in Bartlett, TN for 23 years. A retired dancer, she was the founder of Shimmy Mob Memphis, a chapter of the international organization which raises funds for local domestic abuse shelters around the world.

Today she and her husband live full time in their motorhome and travel the U.S. as she writes her stories. Debra is a travel writer with a travel and RV living blog, Beautiful Day Traveler, where she shares their adventures.

Debra believes "Every day we are alive is a beautiful day.'

For more information about Debra and her books, please visit Debra's website: www.debraparmley.com

ACKNOWLEDGMENTS

Thank you to my writing partner Robert Arrow, and to my sister Kimberly Lear for her genealogy research on our family.

Thank you to Tamara Hoffa our editor, RIP.

Thank you to Sheri McGathy for the beautiful cover, and to Kathryn Faulk for her support.

Infinite love and gratitude to you, my readers.

I treasure you all.

ALSO BY DEBRA PARMLEY

Western Historical Romance:

A Desperate Journey

Dangerous Ties

Deadly Adversaries

Desperate, Dangerous and Deadly: A Western Collection

***

American Mail Order Bride series:

Isabella Bride of Ohio: American Mail Order Brides (co-author Robert Arrow) #17

***

1920's Historical Romance:

Butterflies Fly Free Series:

Trapping the Butterfly: Book One

Dancing Butterfly: Book Two

Exotic Butterfly: Book Three

***

Military Romantic Suspense:

Elle James Brotherhood Protectors world:

Montana Marine

Defensive Instructor

Marine Protector

Marine Protectors Box Set: Montana Marine; Defensive Instructor; and Marine Protector

Blind Trust

A Triple C Ranch Christmas Wedding

Montana Delta Rescue

Montana SEAL Protector

***

Susan Stokers Special Forces Operation Alpha world:

Protecting Pippa

Protecting Zarifah

Split Screen Scream (out of print)

***

Contemporary Romance:

Bobbins Sisters Trilogy:

Check Out, book one

Check In, book two

Aboard the Wishing Star

The Real Movie Hero

Jenna's Christmas Wish

***

Futuristic Romance:

The Hunger Roads Trilogy:

A Change of Scenery (out of print)

Another Change of Scenery: Book One

Down a Back Road: Book Two

Into the Convergence Zone: Book Three

***

Fairy Tale Romance:

The Twelve Stitches of Christmas (co- author Robert Arrow)

Vague Directions

***

Anthologies:

We Know the Truth Do You?

Wounded Heroes Anthology

Hansel and Gretel Anthology

Twilight Dips poetry anthology

Debra Parmley writing as Debra Bishop:

Fairy Tales for all ages: The Sweetest Day

Fantasy: The Rolling House - on Kindle Vella

Children's: coming soon

www.ingramcontent.com/pod-product-compliance
Lightning Source LLC
Chambersburg PA
CBHW030417310726
48979CB00002B/448

* 9 7 8 0 9 9 9 2 5 2 5 7 4 *